LA PETITE MORT

Olivie Blake

WITCH WAY
PUBLISHING

First Printing, 2019

Witch Way Publishing
9090 Skillman St, #182-A/203
Dallas, TX 75243
www.witchwaypublishing.com

Copyright © 2019 by Olivie Blake
Image Copyright © 2019 by Little Chmura

Editor: Tonya Brown
Cover Illustrator: Little Chmura
Cover Designer: Olivie Blake

Printed in the United States of America

ISBN 978-0-578-5552-01

For Tonya and Aurora, my tireless editors,

and for every girl who only smiles to show her teeth.

TABLE *of* CONTENTS

PART I: The Caretaker

"Is this goodbye?" whispered Elisabeth, clinging to the meager fabric of Jacques' shirt. Like the two of them, the garment was torn and dirtied, left to ruin with no promise of mending. "I don't know that I can bear it."

"Goodbye? Never. I'll find you," promised Jacques, gallant in his impossibilities; ever brave, ever clever, ever handsome. They had always known they could never be together—he the penniless rogue, she the forsaken orphan—but in the moment, she longed to believe a different truth. "Whatever it takes, I will make my way to you in the New World, Elisabeth. And if I die trying," he swore,

gathering her in his arms, "then I will have spent my last breath declaring my love for you."

Already, Jacques' quick hands were coveting her bodice; soon, her desire would overtake her will to refuse. "But where will you go? How will you find me?"

"Wherever I have to go. However I have to do it." His certainty stole her breath. "I'll go as far as my feet can take me, Elisabeth; out of Paris, out of France, and into your arms."

His lips, heated with devotion, met hers with the force of a gasp, tangling their bated breaths. This would be goodbye, perhaps forever. She would sail for America tomorrow, leaving her world behind, and as proof of her love, there would be only this: a single, fragile moment of pleasure to last a lifetime.

Desperately, Elisabeth took hold of Jacques'

"Marisa!"

Marisa looked up, startled, as her sister Alicia's elbow landed squarely in her ribs.

"Give me that," Alicia hissed, swatting the book from her hands. "You're going to miss everything—"

"Leese, no," Marisa groaned quietly, struggling to mark her page as Alicia tugged it from her fingers. "Come on, I'm nearly finished, I just want to know how it ends—"

2

"How else? Marriage, babies, happily ever after," Alicia said with a roll of her eyes. "It's a romance book, it's all the same every time!"

"Okay, first of all—"

"—now, all of this is quite silly, of course," their guide was saying loudly, "as in truth, the moniker 'casket girls' is little more than a mistranslation of '*fille à la cassette*,' or 'casquette.' The girls were brought over from France by decree of King Louis XIV in an effort to populate the territory of Louisiana during the early eighteenth century. However, much like the game of telephone, the word 'casquette' soon mutated into the idea that these women were carrying *caskets*—as in, yes, cases for corpses—which was quite sensational to the colonists who lived there. In reality, the casket girls were young women sent to the Ursuline Convent to await a proper husband, but rumor soon spread that the girls had been infected by a particular kind of creature. A *vampire*," the guide finished, leaving space for a dramatic pause, "causing them to crave human blood. Now, as many of you already know, New Orleans is positively steeped in supernatural lore—"

"See? Listen," Alicia said in hushed admonishment, giving Marisa another shove. "It's history, it's interesting, pay attention. You might need to know this someday."

"What on earth would I need to know this for?" Marisa whispered. "They don't make you take a history test to live in New Orleans, Leese, and besides, those girls weren't vampires. The blood thing would have come from tuberculosis—not to mention," she scoffed, "a bunch of young women with no parents, sent to a new country without anyone's protection? They were probably forced into prostitution." She snatched the book back from her sister, concluding, "I'd rather spend my Saturday with Elisabeth and Jacques, thanks."

"Life with a liberal arts major, honestly," Alicia sighed to herself, relinquishing the book with a roll her eyes. "Shouldn't you be fundamentally opposed to romance novels, anyway? Aren't they anti-feminist or something?"

"Don't be ridiculous. The heroines in these books have *agency*, and—"

"Ladies," the tour guide prompted, waiting expectantly for them to look up. "Am I boring you?"

"Sorry, um… Genevieve," Alicia said, squinting down at the gleaming letters of the guide's name badge. "We were just discussing how fascinating this all is. We're Creole," she added, gesturing to herself and Marisa. "Or, you know. Kind of. Our dad is. We were raised in Boston," she clarified, obviously unable to stop

4

herself once she'd started, "but we have family from NOLA. In the French Quarter, actually."

"Interesting," Genevieve said, though she looked fairly unimpressed. "Are you familiar with the French Quarter, then?"

"Oh, no, not at all," Alicia said warmly, always quick to engage with strangers. Probably why *she* was a lawyer, Marisa thought with an internal grumble, while Marisa was mostly adrift. "But my sister just inherited a house there, so, you know. Trying to learn everything we can before she becomes a resident and all that——"

"Well, then I suggest you listen," Genevieve remarked with a mostly-false smile, and Alicia's mouth, which had paused mid-sentence, quietly snapped shut, becoming the stubbornly-set jaw Marisa knew to be far more representative of her combative older sister. "Anyway, as I was saying. The third floor of the convent is where there were supposedly *creatures*, which many have come to believe were vampires——"

"That was totally uncalled for," Alicia muttered to Marisa, irritated now. "You should probably go back to your book while I meditate on not getting into a fight with the snippy tour guide."

"Do you think she's French?" Marisa asked, eyeing Genevieve's features, which now leaned more snobbish than lovely after her retort to Alicia. "I wonder if they pick girls who look French on purpose, just to add to the aesthetic."

"—third floor has windows that were said to be nailed shut," Genevieve went on, her voice slightly raised with each word, "with each nail blessed *by the Pope himself*—"

"You're right, this is stupid," Alicia grumbled to Marisa, glancing around and fidgeting. "Want to get coffee after this? I saw a cute little cafe when we walked over. Something croissant-adjacent, I think."

"Sure," said Marisa, opening her book and resuming her intensive study of what, exactly, Elisabeth was about to desperately do to Jacques.

"Are you sure you can't stay longer?" Marisa lamented, lounging in their hotel room that afternoon after a somewhat exhausting trip down Bourbon Street. "According to Yelp there's some kind of vampire speakeasy somewhere. Since you're so into vampires," she added, rolling over to make a face at Alicia, who sighed.

"I'm not *into* vampires, I just thought, you know, when in NOLA—" She trailed off, frowning at her suitcase. "Did you borrow my bralette?"

"No," Marisa lied, "and are you listening? I don't want you to go. Frankly, I'm a little concerned about what's going to be inside Grandma's house," she said with a shudder. "Dad always said it was cluttered and weird."

"Dad only lived there until he was three," Alicia reminded her, still searching fruitlessly for her clothes. "I think most of what he remembers seeing was in his imagination."

Their father, Luc, had little to say about his New Orleans origins, actually, having lived in Boston nearly all his life. Their grandfather, Lucian, had never spoken on the subject, or about his life in New Orleans at all, until the day he died. All that existed for evidence of the family's Southern past was Marisa's Creole complexion, and a single photograph from their father's birth: baby Luc wrapped up in Oscalia Marrero's arms.

Privately, Marisa had always thought the grandmother she'd never met had a strange look on her face in the picture. Her smile was guarded; almost as if she had seen a ghost somewhere on the other side of the camera lens.

7

"Still," Marisa sighed, flopping onto her back again. "Weird she would leave it to us, isn't it? Considering Dad never even heard from her after Grandpa died."

"Well, she never left her house," Alicia said, adding thoughtfully, "I think she was one of those agoraphobes."

"Ugh. Which means her house is going to be cluttered."

"*Your* house, you mean."

"Ours!"

"Yours," Alicia corrected. "She left it to *one* of the Marrero sisters, not both. It's pretty valuable real estate," she reminded Marisa, still trying to make the best of things. "I looked it up on Zillow and it's worth millions, probably. Or would be, if it had ever been sold—and which I'm selflessly giving up," she teased, knowing full well she had a perfectly sufficient house in Boston and a law career that paid far more than she needed, "so you'll have to stop complaining."

"But—" Marisa sighed. "Can't you at least come with me before tomorrow? I'm going to need help, probably. Boxes and things."

"I wish I could, but unfortunately the partners were pretty clear," Alicia said. "I have to be on a flight tonight."

"Yeah, but—"

"And besides, the will's stipulations are unavoidable." Alicia rose to her feet, falling beside Marisa on the bed. "Weird as it is, you can't enter the premises until the eve of a new moon. So, tomorrow is the earliest." She reached over, tapping Marisa's knuckles fondly. "But I'll be back as soon as I can, promise. And it's not as if you haven't lived alone before, right? Just get a good alarm system and, I don't know. A dog or something."

"Yeah, yeah," Marisa mumbled, feeling immensely childish.

She *had* lived alone, until Paul. And that had been seventeen months of a pretty good thing that abruptly ended along with his MFA program, when he'd packed up for a writing residency somewhere in the woods of the Dakotas. Marisa, who'd never quit the waitressing job she'd taken to pay for her tuition, had found herself out of an apartment and a plan until the day the lawyers informed her family that Oscalia Marrero, the estranged mother of Alicia and Marisa's father Luc, had passed away. Oscalia had left all her belongings, including the house on Royal, not to her son, but to whichever of her two granddaughters was willing to follow her instructions to the letter. Alicia—who was married, taking prenatal vitamins, and on track for a promotion within her firm—

wasn't particularly enticed by the prospect of moving to a totally new city where she knew absolutely no one. Marisa, on the other hand, considered it her personal *Eat, Pray, Love.*

Now that she was actually here, though, she wasn't so sure. She and Alicia had stopped by the previous day to look at the outside of the house, only to find it was so narrow and inauspicious they passed it three consecutive times. Not that Marisa had been expecting to receive one of the beautiful buildings with the trellises and the brick and the charming planters, but the teeny-tiny Creole cottage with its dingy blue shutters and peeling white paint wasn't exactly what she'd hoped to find.

Alicia sighed, rolling over to face Marisa. They were close, despite their five-year age difference, and in spite of the fact that they hardly looked like sisters. Alicia was tiny and petite, with skin that looked permanently tan and hair that, as a child, had been perfect silken ringlets. Marisa, by contrast, was a too-tall, too-thin, hipless and breastless Amazonian with wild, natural hair and a set of hazel eyes that made the question "What *are* you?" the bane of her existence.

"You're going to be fine," Alicia said, patting the top of Marisa's head. "This is your chance to start over, start fresh. Who knows? Maybe you'll actually *have* an adventure instead of just reading about them," she advised, gesturing to the book Marisa had left on the nightstand. "And hey, maybe you'll meet someone."

Despite being a romantic at heart, Marisa wasn't particularly keen to admit it. "Who says I want to meet anyone?"

Alicia gave her a doubtful look.

"I'm working on *me*," Marisa said defensively. Which she was.

Mostly.

"Fine," Alicia permitted, doing Marisa the favor of not voicing her skepticism aloud. "Then at the very least you won't have to pay rent for a year. After that, if you don't like it here, you can always sell the house. We'll figure it out. But in the meantime," she sighed, glancing reluctantly at her watch, "I *do* have to head to the airport, so—"

"You go ahead," Marisa said, not particularly wanting her sister to worry about her. She was, after all, an alleged adult. "I'll just… wander a bit. And I'll FaceTime you tomorrow, after I've gone into the house."

"Perfect." Alicia leaned forward, tapping Marisa's nose. "I've got a really good feeling, you know. I think this is going to be a fun year for you. Besides," she added brightly, "maybe you'll meet a vampire."

"Doubtful," Marisa said. "I'm pretty sure the only bloodsuckers in the Deep South are the mosquitos."

"Well," Alicia replied, "I suppose you'll just have to find out."

Marisa wasn't particularly in the mood for hanging out in an empty hotel room on a Saturday night, so she decided to make her way down Bourbon Street, checking out what would soon be her new home. It was populated mostly by tourists, which was unsurprising, but the whole street had an invigorated feel to it; alive, despite the touted presence of the lingering undead. A trip to Boutique du Vampyre offered up a book about the history of vampires in New Orleans and an invitation to the supposed vampire speakeasy, all which seemed to be part of a kitschy tourist experience Marisa didn't particularly have the energy to fight. In the end, she took the password and the book and wandered over to the bar for a nightcap, still considering it better than being at the hotel alone.

The bar's aesthetic was commendable; the stained glass, the 'break in case of emergency' stake, the attention to detail, the moderately shifty patronage amid people squealing over love potions… it was all very well done, if a bit overwrought. Marisa settled herself in a corner near the balcony, sipping her absinthe cocktail (one would be enough; she could tell as much after a single swallow) and glancing over the book she'd purchased, accidentally knocking shoulders with someone who was passing by.

"Sorry," she said, distractedly shifting for more space.

"Should keep a closer eye on your surroundings," replied a silken female voice, prompting Marisa to look up from the page she'd been reading about a rather monstrous woman named Madame Blanque. "You'll want to be careful around here."

A young woman, hair pulled up in a high ponytail and wearing a pair of skinny black jeans with a velvet tuxedo blazer, was giving Marisa a slow, steady once-over. She wasn't particularly near Marisa's height, bordering on diminutive; with the way her chin was lifted, though, she managed to dominate the space between them, probably owing to the superiority of her clothes. And her shoes. And her face.

The girl's lips slid into a careful, meticulously crafted smile as Marisa blinked, a little taken aback at the attention.

"Why," Marisa asked, and then, in an attempt to joke, "Because of the vampires?"

The girl's hair was an ashy brown-black, her brow a similar darkness, pulled back to reveal a crisply unfurrowed forehead and nose that sloped up from a high bridge. She wore little makeup save for the precise line of her jet black cat-eye and a red lip that was, as Alicia would have probably sniffed, too dark for her ivory complexion. If it weren't for the shape of the girl's mouth (or for that odd smile), she would have looked quite severe. Instead, the upturn of her too-red lips was girlish, a little beauty mark above her mouth lending a sense of innocence to her otherwise unsettling air.

"No," said the girl. "Because men are trash, and at least three of them have been staring at you since you walked in." She angled Marisa slightly to the left, gesturing over her own shoulder. "There's Ed Hardy over there," she said, referencing a man in a deep V-neck who was covered with tattoos, "and Slimeball McGee at six o'clock. Last but not least, there's pale, sweaty white guy," she said, tipping her head to the right, "who looks like the kind of dude to make you think twice about leaving your drink unattended."

"Ah," Marisa said, both relieved and immensely uncomfortable at having their attention pointed out to her. "Thanks, I guess."

"Don't mention it," said the girl, tossing her ponytail over her shoulder and flicking her gaze down to Marisa's book. "Doing homework on a Saturday night?"

"I'm not—" It was obviously a joke, but still, Marisa was a little embarrassed. The girl's teeth slid over her lower lip, obscuring a laugh that made Marisa feel intensely uncool. "I was just, um. Well, nothing really. I just bought it, so—"

"You look familiar," said the girl. "Have we met before?"

"Oh, no, I'm new here, actually," Marisa said. "I'm moving in tomorrow. Are you a local?" she asked, suddenly a little excited at the prospect. "Because, you know, if you are, then—"

"Hey," said a voice, and Marisa was surprised to find Genevieve, the tour guide from the Ursuline Convent, sidling up to the girl and remarking into her ear something that sounded a bit like, "Found a mark."

The girl, whoever she was, appeared to catch Marisa's twitch of a frown. "Her boyfriend Mark," she explained to Marisa, giving Genevieve a nudge. "Gen, meet my new friend…"

She trailed off, waiting for Marisa to take the hint, which she clumsily leapt to do.

"Marisa," she offered quickly, holding out a hand. "You were my tour guide today, actually."

"Oh, right, you," Genevieve said, entirely dispassionate. "Marissa?"

"Ma-*ree*-sa," the other girl corrected, "pay attention."

She slid Marisa another unnerving smile.

"I'm Elisabeth," she said. A common name, though this particular Elisabeth made it less so; as if by possessing it, the phonetics Marisa had heard a million times replaced their prevailing sense of normalcy with new, distinctive features. Sly ones; sharper than normal. "And this is my friend Genevieve, who you seem to know."

"Well, sort of—"

"You ready?" Genevieve interrupted, ignoring Marisa altogether in favor of turning to Elisabeth. Marisa hadn't noticed how young she was until then, registering for the first time that neither Genevieve nor Elisabeth looked any older than she was. They did, however, look *vastly* more sophisticated. Both women were dressed not to make a man weep, but to wonder;

Genevieve's clinging slip dress was paired with a leather jacket, and beneath her fashionably cropped jeans, Elisabeth's ankle booties were lined with studs, the stiletto heel perilously narrow and sharp.

"Damn, you could use those as a weapon," Marisa couldn't help observing aloud, and Elisabeth's gaze caught Marisa's as it traveled up the side of her jeans.

"I have, actually," she said.

Marisa paused, waiting a few beats for a 'just kidding' that never came, then laughed, abruptly apprehensive. "Sorry, I didn't mean to offend you. They're really cool," she said hastily, but to her dismay, Elisabeth seemed to find the remark tiresome. Maybe she'd hoped Marisa would be more refined, like her friend.

Either way, Elisabeth turned to Genevieve. "Yeah, let's go," she said, "I'm hungry."

"Cool," Genevieve replied, giving Marisa a fleeting glance. "Nice meeting you."

"We already met, but you know, yeah. Sure. Bye, then," Marisa said, squirming a little at her own palpable ineptitude. Elisabeth gave her a brisk, parting nod, but before she had fully turned away, she sent Genevieve on ahead, hanging back to lean towards Marisa.

"Seriously, be careful," Elisabeth murmured to her. "Can't just go around reading books alone in bars."

"Got nowhere better to read them, I guess," Marisa joked, still unforgivably awkward, and Elisabeth arched a brow.

"You know, I used to read a lot myself. Learned kind of late in life," Elisabeth explained, "so it was a bit of an addiction for a time; like I was looking for something. Searching, I guess. Now, though, I find it difficult to focus for an entire story. At this point," she concluded with a listless shrug, "reading's a lot like cigarettes."

"What, lethal?" Marisa asked.

"No." Elisabeth smiled thinly. "Best enjoyed after sex."

Then, before Marisa could process what she'd said, she'd added, "See you around, maybe," and turned away, following a waiting Genevieve.

Marisa shook herself of the encounter, watching the two girls wander over to two men Genevieve seemed to know. One was probably Mark, Marisa reasoned, while the other, a hot but douchey-looking dudebro with a fake tan, was clearly reserved for Elisabeth. She reached up, greeting him with a brush of her red lips to his cheek, and Marisa shivered, suddenly keenly aware of her own skin; as if, somewhere, she could feel her own blood pumping through her veins, thrilling through her limbs to set every hair on end.

Odd, she thought, and finished her drink, setting the empty glass down.

She really, really ought to get some sleep.

At about six in the evening of the first day of the new moon—after checking out of her hotel and lugging four suitcases' worth of things into a Lyft and then out onto the street—Marisa stood on the threshold of her new old house, instructions in hand. Her grandmother's attorney, a man she'd never met who communicated purely through email, had sent her the code to a lockbox and a reminder: *A Marrero daughter must step, with both feet, onto the other side of the threshold on the day of the new moon.*

Marisa sighed, glancing up at the peeling paint. This would be a fixer-upper, whether she wanted to sell it or keep it. It seemed Oscalia Marrero had lived beyond the point where she could reasonably keep up with the house's maintenance, which left Marisa to dread what sort of nightmare scenario was likely to be inside. She opened the lockbox, withdrew the single key, and placed it in the lock.

To her surprise, though, the latch seemed to give way the moment she touched the door, leaning against the wood. The key, meanwhile, had embedded itself into the lock, wedged in without hope of withdrawal before promptly disappearing.

Marisa frowned. It seemed she'd have to call a locksmith, too, in addition to painters.

She paused, as instructed, with both feet on the threshold, and then reached over to turn on the lights, finding that there was no switch. Despite this, a lamp across the foyer turned on and, with a little gasp-hiccup of surprise—after nearly falling backwards—she watched the rooms beyond the entryway became illuminated in full, one by one, by Victorian sconces that led out of sight.

"Yeesh," Marisa said, shaking herself and pulling her luggage in after her. "Creepy."

Past the foyer was a set of glass doors, opening to a surprisingly large kitchen and dining area, which then led to a living room. To her surprise, the interior structure was high-ceilinged and impossibly large; she half wanted to run back outside and take another look at the house's facade, just to try to determine how any of this was possible. Short of that, though, Marisa ran her fingers over an old Steinway piano, which hardly possessed any dust, and took in the contents of the first floor: a series of densely-occupied mahogany shelves; a porcelain bust of what looked like a European woman, possibly French or Italian; a portrait of an eighteenth-century noble; a white painted mantle, above which was an ornate brass mirror; a set of high-backed velvet chairs; a collection of copper pots, all which hung from above; and an enormous crystal chandelier, which, like the foyer lamp, did not seem to have a light switch or any wiring.

Marisa wandered back to the foyer, leaving her suitcases behind, and made her way up the stairs. There was a bedroom suite, including a massive four-poster bed, and a bathroom with one of those clawfoot tubs; no shower. The wardrobe, to her surprise, was empty. Someone must have been there after her grandmother died; it was almost as if the house had been cleaned and emptied in advance, only her lawyer had already made it clear that under no circumstances had another human being been allowed inside the house before the evening of the new moon.

Marisa paused beside a set of narrow stairs leading from the small balcony of the bedroom to an outer courtyard, which she realized with a start connected the house to an additional building; a guest house, presumably, though it was hardly a cottage. Instead, the addition to the house was a multistory, nearly free-standing structure with a series of accessible doors, like a motel. She wandered down the steps, reaching the courtyard's cobbled ground, and reached for the nearest of the guest house's doors.

This one wouldn't open. She jiggled the knob, but nothing. No hole for a key, either.

She frowned, contemplating who to call about this. The lawyer hadn't left any instructions, and she hadn't seen anything inside the house. How was anyone supposed to access any of the rooms? What had they been used for? She turned back to the stairs, resuming her path to the house to reread the email from the lawyer for the thirtieth time.

As she was stepping into the foyer, though, she stopped, spying an umbrella on the polished brass coat rack that she was quite certain hadn't been there when she'd come in.

"Hello?" she called, anxiety flaring up in her chest as she noticed the glass doors to the kitchen, slightly ajar, were definitely not how she'd left them. "I should warn you, I have a—"

She broke off, leaping back as a man, tall and wearing a black coat with an upturned collar, glanced up from where he was making a sandwich.

"A what?" he prompted.

"A… gun," Marisa lied.

"You don't have a gun," the man said. He was more than tall, on second glance; he had a linear sort of look to him, lean and polished, and appeared to be somewhere in his thirties. His hair, a mahogany not unlike the living room's shelves, shone auburn in the light; it fell in a loose, swooping curl onto his forehead, which he brushed aside with the back of his wrist. His nose was narrow, cheeks shadowed with a faint degree of facial hair, and his eyes were a bright and gleaming blue.

Confusingly, he asked, "Where's Oscalia?"

"Who are you?" countered Marisa, who was still not entirely sure she shouldn't call the police. "How'd you get in?"

"I have a key, in a sense," he replied, taking a bite of his sandwich, "and I'm Jack. Are you a friend of Oscalia's?"

"I'm Oscalia's granddaughter," Marisa said, and Jack promptly dropped the sandwich, letting it fall to the plate as he stared at her. "I'm Marisa," she added, on the off-chance he'd recognize her name; he seemed to have known her grandmother, though she couldn't imagine how.

"No," he said to something that didn't seem to be her, sounding somewhere between concerned and

23

disbelieving. "I thought you looked familiar, but——" He shook himself. "A blood relative?" he prompted, interrogating her now. "A direct descendant?"

"Yes, I told you, I'm her grand-"

"Well, then it's a good thing I found you before the others arrive," said Jack, waving a hand. Immediately, the sandwich disappeared, and Marisa stared at where it had been, blinking. He caught her gaze, commenting flippantly, "Oh, stop. Basically a party trick. I take it your grandmother didn't leave any instructions, then?"

"I... Well, I have the code to the lockbox," Marisa said, still staring at the vacancy that had once been sandwich. "That," she recalled suddenly, glancing up, "and that I had to enter with both feet in the threshold, which I have to assume is my grandmother's sense of humor or something——"

Abruptly, Jack's expression took on a ripple of concern.

"Oh, this isn't good at all. You have no idea, do you?" he asked her, abandoning the sandwich altogether and sweeping forward to reach her side. There was a faint smell of something like licorice to him, reminding Marisa briefly of the absinthe she'd had the night before. He had an earthy sort of scent, with a splash of something soothing. Pine, she guessed, settled crisply beneath the anise smell; which she could identify, a little breathlessly, only because he stood quite unnervingly close.

"You've just done something incredibly foolish," he murmured, giving her a look of such palpable concern that it raised her gaze slowly to his.

"What?" she asked, slightly dizzied.

He considered her for a solemn moment; a grave one, in fact. Serious looked well on him, though she doubted anything looked particularly poor. His blue eyes were intensely bright, and she found herself struggling to look at him without blatantly staring.

"Listen carefully," he told her, "because I'd like to only say this once. Your grandmother was what's called a Caretaker," he explained, and she blinked. Whatever she'd expected, this wasn't it. "There has been one in the French Quarter for over a century, and it is passed through the members of your bloodline. Now, this is the important part: You have just completed the new moon ritual," he informed her. "You accepted your position when you stepped into your blood's inheritance, standing on the threshold with both feet. Legally speaking, a contract has been made. You are now responsible for the creatures under your care; you may not turn them away, and you must house them. So long as you call this house your home, you will not be harmed by them. However, should you ever attempt to leave, the contract is broken, and those creatures may seek vengeance on the Caretaker who denied them keeping."

"Now," he continued, clearing his throat, "as for who I am, it's… a longer story. But suffice it to say, I am Jack St. Germaine," he said, bowing low in introduction, "and I'm a witch. An alchemist, actually, and therefore a scientist. Any questions?"

That was certainly a name she wished had been less familiar. Unfortunately, given her evening of recreational New Orleans research, she could have given a full report on any number of names; Delphine LaLaurie, who had tortured dozens of people in her house; the Casket Girls, who had come over from France and taken residence in the Ursuline Convent; and, of course—

"St. Germaine the vampire?"

Famous for being handsome, mysterious, extravagantly wealthy, and… ah yes, for the woman who had jumped from his balcony screaming that he was going to drink her blood, right before he vanished overnight.

That St. Germaine? He didn't seem particularly bloodthirsty; nor, Marisa supposed, did he enjoy being asked if he was.

"I'm not a vampire, I'm an *alchemist*," he told her again, looking a bit exasperated that she hadn't been properly listening. "And before you ask, no, I had no intention of drinking that woman's blood. That story is nothing more than an unfortunate misunderstanding."

"Which part did she misunderstand?" Marisa asked warily, and Jack gave a heavy sigh.

"The point is, this city is positively enraptured with vampires," he said, discarding her question entirely, "but not everyone can be an undead creature of the night, can they? Some of us are simply historians, musicians, authors, artists—"

"How many of you are there?"

"I was simply listing my own professions," he said curtly, "but if you must know, then perhaps a hundred total within the city. Others exist regionally, of course, and there are those traveling between districts, which you will have to tend to—"

"And why should I believe you?" Marisa asked, a little numbed by the idea that a man had broken into her house, managed to construct a sandwich despite there being no food in the fridge, and then claimed to be some sort of witch before telling her she'd been unwillingly employed as a hotelier for monsters.

"Well, mostly because you have very little choice," said Jack, confirming her suspicions, just before they heard a knock from somewhere in the house. "Going to get that?" he prompted, the sandwich abruptly resuming its position in his hand, and Marisa glanced over her shoulder at the front door, more than a little concerned about who that could be.

"I don't really know if I should—"

"It's not that door," Jack informed her, unhelpfully amused.

Marisa opened her mouth to retort something about what other door it could possibly be when her feet began traveling without her permission, one hand landing on the courtyard door before she fully registered she'd moved.

She could feel the latch giving way at her touch, the door flying open to reveal a wiry, haggard-looking man, his clothing stained and torn.

"I need a room," he said, his voice a gruff, nearly incoherent Southern accent that ended with him licking his chops (was that possible for a man to do?) and pawing irritably at the wood of the threshold.

"Um," managed Marisa, repulsed by the smell of what seemed to be raw meat. "Well, I don't... I'm not sure if—"

"Rougarou," Jack murmured in her ear, startling her as he leaned into the threshold from behind her, resting one hand on the beam of the door. "Something like a Cajun variety of werewolf. Surely you've heard?"

She hadn't—it was probably in tonight's pages on the mythos of New Orleans, assuming Marisa didn't miraculously become less mundane and pass up reading in favor of whatever other adults did on the weekends— but that didn't seem worth pointing out. "But I can't open the doors," she said, frowning, and the rougarou made a growling sound of displeasure, teeth snapping as he waited.

"Well, you couldn't before," Jack agreed, "but now…"

He trailed off, gesturing her to the closest of the guest house doors. She gave him a small glare, then wandered over, the rougarou stumbling at her heels. This time, when she touched her hand to the knob, she heard the latch release, the hinges creaking open to reveal the interior of a dark room.

"Oh," she said, moving to step inside with curiosity, but Jack's hand closed around her forearm, holding her back.

"It's not for you," he warned, as the rougarou shoved past them and slammed the door shut, the shutters from both floors of the guest house giving a wheezing thwack. "Do you see what I mean about being a Caretaker?" Jack said, easing her back toward the house.

"Well, do they pay me or something?" she asked, and then, to his arched brow of *very funny, princess*, she sighed, "What is this, Hotel Transylvania?"

"Ha," said Jack, "*no*. It's more like a youth hostel, only for creatures in need. They'll mostly leave you alone," he added, gesturing to the rougarou's room. "But, obviously, the caretaking aspect is very minimal. You mostly just open the doors."

"That's it?"

"That's it," Jack said, nodding. "The French Quarter used to be a safe place for creatures, but no longer. You're their only method of safe passage, and now that you've accepted the house, you're bound to its rules."

The idea of being trapped inside a house for the purpose of sheltering various forms of the undead struck Marisa as very unsteadying indeed.

"I think I need a drink," Marisa muttered, and Jack smiled slowly.

"I know precisely where to get one," he said.

"Where are we going?"

"A little place I know," he said. His pace was measured and easy, and she, long-legged creature that she was, was forced to match his languid stride with pained deliberation. "One might call it a speakeasy."

"Oh, I've been there," Marisa said, and Jack paused to sigh, giving her a doubtful glance.

"You mean that vampire nest with the tourists and the little roaming familiars?" he sniffed, sounding a bit uppity in his opposition. "That's hardly what I had in mind."

Rather, what Jack had in mind was underground, sunk beneath a building Marisa hadn't noticed before. Venturing down the spiral stairs was eerily similar to the speakeasy from the previous night; a perfectly symmetrical reflection, in fact, but where one establishment resided on an upper floor with a balcony, this stairwell led to a dark and cavernous underground.

"The one you went to was inspired by this one," Jack explained, knocking on the door, "though the demographic varies slightly."

"Between?" Marisa prompted.

"Look, you're going to hear me say this a lot, but it's really better if you don't know," Jack said.

A slat in the wood opened, revealing a set of luminous grey eyes.

"Password?" prompted a slippery voice.

"It's Jack," said Jack.

"That's not the password."

"Well, I've just gotten into town," Jack replied smoothly, "and haven't had a chance to check in on Aguillard. But, if you'd like, I could make this door not a door."

There was a pause.

"Welcome home, you bastard," grumbled the voice, and then the door opened, revealing—as Marisa had suspected—a mirror-image of the speakeasy she'd visited before, although the eyes and voice that had been at the door were nowhere to be seen.

"Come on," Jack said, giving her a nudge to the bar.

This establishment, unlike the other, wasn't particularly busy. The bar was occupied by a few empty chairs and two men in suits talking quietly, though they

looked up as she approached. They gave her a wary
stare and then, noticing Jack, plucked their drinks from
the bar, rising to their feet. No words were exchanged,
but they both nodded politely, almost deferentially.

Jack, whoever he was, was clearly someone people
knew.

"Whiskey neat," Jack said to the bartender, who
looked human enough. "Two."

Marisa was about to argue that she'd never liked her
whiskey neat and certainly had no plans to drink it now,
but she felt the effort would be wasted. Instead, she slid a
glance around the room, taking in the strange world of
the supernatural underground.

"Don't stare," warned Jack.

"I'm not," she said, though she was, and in fact, she
had a right to be. Particularly when she noticed that in a
corner of the bar, precisely where she would have been if
this were upside-down and yesterday, there was the girl,
Elisabeth, whom she'd met the night before.

That evening, Elisabeth was wearing a fitted black
shirt with a plunging back, her calf-length skirt of black
chiffon floating down to give her a sleekly pulled-
together silhouette. Beside her were two other young
women, both in tailored black clothing; all three were

33

engaged in a heated argument with someone sitting out of sight.

"I thought I told you not to—" Jack stiffened, following Marisa's line of sight to Elisabeth. "Stare," he finished, and moved on brusquely to, "What's she doing here? She's not allowed in."

"Why not?" Marisa asked, glancing at him. "Is she not, you know. A creature?"

She must have sounded a little too foolishly optimistic. Jack's brow furrowed, registering, correctly, that Marisa had met Elisabeth before.

"You know her?" he asked, and Marisa shook her head quickly.

"No, not really, I just—"

"Good. Stay away from her," Jack warned, his face taking on a look she hadn't seen from him yet. "Unlike me, Elisabeth Clavier *is* a vampire, and a dangerous one, at that."

Perhaps it said a lot about Marisa's current state that her first thought, rather than scoffing about vampires not being real, was to find it retroactively unsurprising that Elisabeth had been so derisive about the book.

Then, belatedly, Marisa frowned, registering something more pressing about what Jack had just informed her. "I thought you said creatures couldn't harm me?"

"I didn't say they couldn't," he corrected. "I said they *wouldn't*, but Elisabeth isn't like other vampires. She and her sisters hunt mortals for sport. How did you meet her?"

A bit incongruous, transitioning from murder accusations to small talk, but Jack had hardly stopped for breath.

"At that bar," Marisa said, adding, "You know, the vampire speakeasy that's not a vampire speakeasy," when Jack stiffened. "So she's a real vampire, then?" Marisa pressed him, confused. "But I thought you said creatures don't go th-"

"She wasn't there for a *drink*, Marisa. Or, well, she was," Jack corrected himself, bristling as he glanced in Elisabeth's direction again, "but certainly not the kind with absinthe."

Marisa stifled a sense of revulsion, recalling the way Elisabeth's red lips had pressed to the man's cheek. Unluckily, it was in that precise moment that Elisabeth looked up, finding Marisa across the bar.

Even from a distance, it was difficult not to notice the change in the thin line of Elisabeth's unnerving mouth, irritation from her clandestine argument suddenly falling away. It became a narrow-eyed look of suspicion, directed first at Jack, and then a look of curiosity as it traveled slowly to Marisa's.

Ultimately, Elisabeth's gaze settled on hers, landing with a look of—

Marisa shivered. *Hunger* would be the word, but she hoped that was only her imagination.

"She's not allowed in here," Jack said again, fingers tight around his glass of whiskey. "She doesn't follow the rules."

"What rules?"

"No recreational hunting," he said stiffly. "No turning on others of her kind."

"Other vampires?"

"Yes," he said. "And other things, too." He glanced over his shoulder, looking for someone. "I should talk to Aguillard about this; he should know Elisabeth's crossing lines again. Wait here," he instructed Marisa, who immediately (and rightfully) balked.

"I'm not staying *here*—"

"You'd rather go home by yourself?" Jack asked doubtfully, and Marisa winced, thinking of the werewolf in her guest house, along with whatever else might be waiting upon her return.

"No," she admitted, "but—"

"Then *stay here*," Jack said, rising to his feet. "I'll be right back."

He rose without further comment, making his way towards a panel in the wall that appeared to be a door. She watched him disappear behind it, then reached out, clinging to her glass of whiskey like a security blanket. She downed half a gulp, pulling a face as it burned unpleasantly down her throat.

She hazarded another glance over her shoulder after a moment, her gaze drifting with morbid curiosity to where Elisabeth had been, but found that all three women had vanished. Whoever they'd been speaking to was gone now, too, with only empty air remaining where they'd been. Marisa shivered, then leapt with alarm when the bartender slammed another drink down, this time for a beady-eyed man one stool over.

Marisa rose to her feet, nearly toppling in place. "Bathroom?" she said to the bartender, who pointed with a grunt. She nodded, shielding her purse tightly under her arm as she slipped into the corridor.

Luckily, the bathroom was empty, and Marisa made her way to the mirror. Same big hair, which Louisiana's humidity certainly wasn't helping. Same eyes, only they were wide and frightened now, like a child's. She swallowed, hoping to calm herself, and turned to enter

37

the stall, emitting half a shriek as she realized someone was standing in front of the door.

"So," said Elisabeth Clavier, smiling her darkly innocent smile. "You're the new Caretaker, huh?"

"I—" Marissa swallowed hard. Would Jack hear her if she screamed? Would *anyone* hear her? "Elisabeth, I, um—"

She broke off as Elisabeth strode forward, backing her against the lip of the sink. The ceramic dug into Marisa's low back, pressing warningly into her spine, and she felt her heart race, pulsing violently in her throat.

Elisabeth's dark gaze dropped to Marisa's neck, lingering there.

"There are some things you should know," Elisabeth murmured, still watching the thrum of Marisa's pulse. Run-*run*, run-*run*, only it was fruitless. Marisa was rooted in place, unable to move. "First of all, I can go wherever I like. Secondly—and listen closely," she cautioned, "because this is important—"

She leaned forward, her breath skating coolly over the pulse at Marisa's neck until the air in Marisa's own lungs turned painful, forming a hard knot inside her throat.

"Jack St. Germaine is not to be trusted," Elisabeth warned in her ear, the words like ice against Marisa's veins.

Then, before Marisa could say a word, Elisabeth had disappeared, leaving only traces of pebbled gooseflesh for evidence of where she'd been.

PART II: The Alchemist

Despite the fact that Jack St. Germaine wasn't technically a creature (and, more importantly, he had never met a locked door that wouldn't open for at least one of his persuasive qualities), Oscalia Marrero, former Caretaker, had once given him a key for his own room. He asked her why, naturally, but she'd offered little in explanation. She was getting on in age by then, and sometimes mumbled things to herself that sounded more like spells than conversation. On the occasion of the key's impartment, for example, Jack had managed to grasp only one thing that came out of Oscalia's mouth.

"Come," she said, "and see what the new moon brings you."

She'd said it with closed eyes, as if she were reading him something from a book that only she could see. Some years later, Oscalia would eventually go blind, and by then Jack had already developed a habit of returning to New Orleans for a single night on the eve of a new moon. The city had not been his home for a long time; in fact, he had not considered himself to have a home at all for many decades. He preferred it that way, as people like him weren't built for permanence, even when (*especially* when) they outlasted everything else.

But it was occurring to him now that he might have no other choice but to stay beyond his usual duration.

"Why is she here?" Jack demanded of Aguillard, the Creole bar owner who, per usual, sat behind his ornate desk. Together, Jack and Aguillard were considered the leaders of the New Orleans creature community, though in general Jack preferred not to interfere, as he didn't care to micromanage.

Except when it came to Elisabeth, of course; but that, as far as Jack was concerned, was a *management* problem, with nothing remotely 'micro' about it.

"I presume she's here because the previous Caretaker passed on," Aguillard lazily replied, "though I would have thought you'd know as much already."

"Not Marisa," Jack corrected impatiently, referring to the girl he'd just met, who was evidently Oscalia's granddaughter. "Elisabeth."

As in, Elisabeth Clavier, diminutive vampiress and murder enthusiast.

It should have been obvious from the outset which woman he meant, but to Jack's displeasure, Aguillard was again playing a game he had recently come to enjoy, which was coincidentally a torment Jack deeply despised. It typically involved one of them pretending not to know what the other was talking about until the other grew impatient and began cursing things.

The first move was usually feigned oblivion.

"You mean the Casket Girl?" asked Aguillard.

"Don't pretend you don't know perfectly well who I mean," Jack said, tapping a foot in agitation. "You may recall, Aguillard, that Elisabeth is supposed to be—oh, I don't know," he mused facetiously, "banished?"

Banished was an old word, but a good one.

"So yes, the Casket Girl," Aguillard confirmed pointedly, casting an irreverent glance askance at Jack. "You're proof enough that banishment is hardly permanent, aren't you, Jack? And besides, I hardly owe her my attention beyond what is necessary."

"Well, you'd better pay attention now, because she's here," Jack said, "and from the sounds of it, she's going after the new Caretaker. Elisabeth and Oscalia coexisted at best," he growled under his breath, "but if Elisabeth wins over Marisa—"

Gratifyingly, Jack didn't have to finish his sentence, as Elisabeth Clavier winning anything was a troubling enough outcome that even Aguillard's little game couldn't abide it. The prospect of the new Caretaker being swayed by the Casket Girls, and by Elisabeth in particular, was a distressing one. It would upset the balance of power in immortal New Orleans, and if there was one thing nature (and the unnatural) didn't care for, it was imbalance of any sort.

"Oscalia was always pleasantly neutral," Aguillard remarked, adding thoughtfully, "And you didn't tell the girl everything, did you?"

"Of course not," Jack snapped. "I'm not an idiot."

"Could have fooled me. After all, the solution here is rather straightforward, isn't it? Simply don't let Elisabeth sway her," Aguillard suggested. He had the airs of a Southern gentleman, always mere breaths away from placing a pipe between his lips or divining his luck with

44

the ponies. "Or are you so insecure these days you no longer think yourself capable of retaining her interests?"

Jack grimaced. "Listen, I like the girl well enough—"

"Like her, dislike her, what difference is that to me?" Aguillard asked, shrugging. "We have an agreement, Jack."

"I wouldn't call it that," Jack muttered, bristling.

"And yet I just did," Aguillard replied.

Jack tightened a fist, irritated. He was beginning to remember why he'd left New Orleans in the first place.

"Hm," Aguillard commented unhelpfully, "and here I thought it was your Casket Girl who'd run you out."

Jack, predictably, scowled.

"Stop doing that." When Aguillard smiled thinly, Jack added, "You do realize what she's capable of, don't you? That little mind-reading parlor trick of yours won't help any of us if Elisabeth gets Marisa on her side, and without me—"

"Without you," Aguillard supplied coolly, "I have nothing, Jack, just as you have nothing without me. So, can't we both agree to do our jobs, then? Assuming you plan to stay," he added, "which, frankly, I could take or leave, seeing as you seem to have lost your touch."

"I haven't lost it." Jack thought of Marisa—of her long limbs and her wild hair and her curiously amber eyes—and shook his head. "But I need you to keep a better eye on your establishment, Aguillard, because if you expect to come up against Elisabeth and win, then you're going to need to seal the cracks."

"Worry about your own cracks, St. Germaine," Aguillard advised, and though Jack's temper threatened to get the better of him again, Aguillard merely plucked a speck of invisible dust from his jacket. "Relax," he said, presumably to Jack. "Elisabeth's just here to settle a debt. I gave her ten minutes," he added, glancing down at his watch, "nine of which she spent on threats, and one of which she just used intimidating your new pet."

At the reminder of Marisa being left unattended, Jack blinked. "Fuck," he muttered, pivoting on his heel. "And she's not my pet," he snapped at a chuckling Aguillard before transferring through the wall of the office, colliding with Marisa on the other side.

"What did she say?" he demanded, and Marisa retreated half a step, startled.

"What did who say?" she replied once she'd recovered, not very convincingly, and Jack sighed, gesturing for her to follow him as he hastily led her out of the bar.

"I know Elisabeth talked to you," he warned, probably too-sharply, catching the tell-tale discomfort on

Marisa's face at the mention of Elisabeth. He hoped that was a promising sign; proving, at least, that whatever Elisabeth had tried to do, she probably hadn't managed it.

Unfortunately, Marisa now seemed less willing to meet his eye than she had before, which wasn't particularly reassuring.

"Hey," Jack sighed, pausing Marisa on the stairs, "listen to me." He rested a hand on her shoulder, attempting some form of comfort; he'd had a way with women once. More than once; for every woman that ran from his house screaming, there were dozens more who'd happily spent the night. "Elisabeth is a born liar. Persuasive."

When Marisa still seemed reluctant to face him, he softened even further, gingerly drawing her gaze up. "She was like that even before she turned," he explained, "and believe me, you're not the first to be taken in."

That got Marisa's attention. "Before she was…" Marisa trailed off, obviously struggling to process that information. "You knew her before she was a vampire?"

"We knew each other once, a long time ago. In France."

He didn't particularly want to get into it. It was a long story, and not one he enjoyed telling. Particularly

47

not in the stairwell of a creature bar, where even the walls had eyes.

Regrettably, Marisa's brow furrowing suggested she planned to press him.

"Does that mean—"

"You should probably know," Jack cautioned the newest Caretaker, "that not all vampires are created equal. Partially because they're made, not born, and because while they all have some degree of extraordinary ability—speed, persuasion, telepathy," he clarified, as Marisa gave a wary nod, "the concentration of powers they have after they're turned depends on what they were before. Elisabeth was never innocent," Jack warned, "and she always has an agenda."

Marisa's doubtful expression didn't shift. "And what's your agenda, then?"

"Mine?" Jack echoed. He hadn't expected to become part of the equation so quickly, though he supposed it was unsurprising that Elisabeth had made him one. She did, after all, resent him for a large number of things, most of them undeserved.

Well. *Some* of them undeserved, anyway. "You think I want something from you?"

"You obviously do," Marisa said, rolling her eyes. "It's not like the St. Germaine legend is notorious for its altruistic hero."

"Well, history is written by the victors," Jack said. "In this case, the vampires."

Marisa frowned. "But—"

"You don't have to trust me yet," Jack assured her, mostly because it had become apparent that she wasn't going to. "You don't know me, and that's fine. But for now, I can keep you safe. If you want to know what this town is really like, you'll need my help."

That seemed to get through to her; perhaps she'd noticed the sort of deference he got from other creatures, or remembered he'd been there to help her with the one already in the house. Either way, she sighed, conceding, and when Jack gestured up towards the street, she finally gave a conciliatory nod, taking the first step, and then the second.

"Well, wait," she said, doubling-back on their progress (much to his dismay) to pause him before continuing up the stairs. "One more thing. When we got here, you said you'd just gotten into town." She hesitated, then asked, "What brought you back?"

Jack looked up at where she stood, considering her. Had there been any glow from the street above, her wild hair might have softened around her like a halo; he considered that perhaps such a view might have swayed him unreasonably, given the artistry of her composition.

Luckily, there was no need to be concerned. He was easily bedded, not readily swayed, and artistically-speaking, the stairway was dark and unenticing.

"New moons," Jack said, gesturing to the vacancy of sky, "are for new beginnings."

Marisa's eyes narrowed. "That's not an answer."

"No," he agreed, "it isn't," and though he'd been concerned she might still argue, she simply shrugged and carried on, taking the remainder of the stairs to return to her grandmother's house.

"There's something weird about this house, isn't there?" Marisa asked Jack, like a child afraid to go to sleep in the dark. "I can't get over the fact that there's a werewolf in my guest house. Assuming he's even the only one," she grumbled, and Jack shook his head.

"He is, because you're the one who lets them in," he reminded her.

"What if I missed someone while we were gone?"

"You'd have known."

"How?"

"I don't know. Oscalia never told me the details."

Not exactly a lie, though not a full truth, either. Certainly Oscalia had never told him, and even if she had ever really understood it herself, he doubted she ever suspected he did. She could never have known how much he actually knew, or else she would have done something about it.

Something his life rather depended on; not that Marisa needed to know that.

"Oh," Marisa said, looking uncomfortable, which was something Jack found immensely relatable. It was like an organ transplant; some new ability her body would likely fight at first. He'd felt the same way, once upon a time. "So, I can't, you know. Get a job, or… anything?"

"You don't need one," Jack said. "The house will provide whatever you need."

"Oh, really?" Marisa scoffed. "So it'll pay my taxes? Give me health insurance?"

"You won't get sick. I told you, the house will care for you."

"My grandmother died," Marisa pointed out, and Jack shook his head.

51

"She passed," he corrected, "and because we have no knowledge of the alternatives, we *assume* that she died."

Marisa shuddered, glancing around at the walls. "Well, that's another layer of creepy I could have done without."

"It is what it is," Jack advised, finishing his nightcap and vanishing the glass. "Now, if you don't mind, I'm off to bed, so—"

"How do you do that?" Marisa asked, gesturing to the empty air where the glass had been. She, like most mortals, was entranced by even the smallest magics. Jack had enjoyed that reaction of wide-eyed wonder once upon a time, delighting in the allure of his talent; unfortunately, outside the convenience of tending to household drudgery, his abilities had since lost most of their appeal.

And quite a bit of their effectiveness, too.

"I was apprenticed to a witch when I was young," he said. "I learned from him."

"But you said you were an alchemist," Marisa said, bemused, and Jack shrugged.

"Because I am, primarily." He certainly was now. "Any talent can be developed if you pursue it long enough. Of course, I do have some natural ability," he assured her, gesturing to his hands. "When I was a youth, I was preternaturally lucky. It was a spark of witchery that grew over time, but I managed most of my accomplishments on my own—via alchemy."

"Lucky?" she asked, still not entirely clear, and he nodded.

"Luck is a forgettable magic, because it looks quite like probability," he explained. "But then, isn't that all magic is? Making the unlikely more likely can equally reveal itself in clever guesses, intuitive decisions. Chance meetings, for example," he murmured, and watched a little more warmth invade the dusky color of her skin.

She hid it well, or tried to, clearing her throat and flashing him a skeptical look. "Are all chance meetings lucky?"

"In my case? Yes," Jack said.

"Could I learn it, like you did?"

"Provided you had enough time, I suppose it depends. Do you have any magic now?" he asked her, and she frowned, pensive.

"No," she said eventually. "I don't think so."

Good, he thought, better that you think that. Perhaps you'll make it true.

"Well, there's no shame in mortality." He rolled out his neck with palpable exhaustion, turning his attention to the guest house. "Anyway, I'm off to bed, so—"

"What happened to him?" Marisa interrupted. "The witch," she clarified, when Jack turned to look at her. "The one you were apprenticed to?"

A question, he thought, that history would never tire of asking.

"He lived forever in infamy," Jack said, "which is to say, he died. Goodnight," he added, and before Marisa could ask more questions—something she surely intended to do—he slipped out through the kitchen doors, making his way to his usual room.

Jack spent most of the following day running his usual errands. A favorite of his more menial tasks was bringing a reasonable amount of alchemically manufactured gold to his usual pawn shop, which was something he typically did on a monthly basis. By now, the owner knew better than to ask questions, and besides, Jack was pretty sure she had been a dragon in her past life. She seemed pleased enough by anything that glittered without having to ask about its source.

After the pawn shop was the tailor, as Jack preferred his clothing bespoke. He was taller than the average man, broader shouldered, with a longer torso and still-longer legs. This, too, was something he could conceivably do by himself, but why waste whatever magic he had left? He appreciated the walk between errands, stepping contentedly out of the pawn shop and into the sun to make his way down the street.

"You know," remarked someone to his left, nearly startling him into dropping his wallet, "counterfeit would really be much easier, Jack. This place is clean across town from the Caretaker's house."

He bit back the urge to heartily profane as Elisabeth Clavier dropped her sunglasses, lowering them just enough to deliver the regrettable sight of her dark eyes. As usual, her lips twisted up with something too wicked to be mirth, though she was wearing a pair of jeans, a striped Breton top, and pristine ballet flats, which was hardly her usual style. Jack guessed she was costumed as a normal person; forgettable until she decided not to be. The last thing he wanted to do was let her believe she'd startled him.

"I like to stretch my legs from time to time," he said.

"True," she sighed, all coquetry and floaty innocence. "And your golden age of killing demons is long behind you, isn't it?"

Her knowledge of his history was always so disquieting.

"It was one demon," he reminded her, "and I learned my lesson."

"Well, have to get your exercise in somehow," Elisabeth remarked, letting her gaze focus so intently on his stomach that he fought the urge to fold his arms over his chest. She smiled at his discomfort, and then let her attention rise to his face again. "Strange you don't look happy to see me," she commented, meeting his scowl with a smile. "What are you doing back in New Orleans, if not for me?"

"I live here, Elisabeth. Despite your best efforts."

"Oh, please." He didn't need to see behind her lenses to know she'd rolled her eyes. "You're flattering yourself if you think those were my best efforts."

This would go on all day if he let her. She wasn't unlike Aguillard that way, though at least Aguillard always acted alone. If Elisabeth wasn't up to something where Jack could see it, the likelihood increased exponentially that one of her sisters was misbehaving out of sight.

"What's to keep me from killing you now?" he asked her, flicking a pointed glance to the amulet she wore on her finger. "All I'd need is to remove that and the sun would do it for me, even without my help."

"Yes, true you could," Elisabeth agreed, shrugging, "but then our little chat would be over, and we all know you'd rather die than stop chasing my shadow all over town."

Jack sighed, resuming his path to the tailor. "What do you want?" he asked, hating the way she so naturally fell in step with him. "We were doing so well at avoiding each other. What has it been, five years? Ten?"

"Honestly, time is so difficult to keep track of I've simply stopped bothering," Elisabeth replied. "Though, as far as I'm concerned, you're the one who's been showing up uninvited, not me."

That prompted the recollection of her appearance from the night before, gifting Jack another nameless sense of prophecy.

"What disagreement did you have at the bar?" he asked her, sparing a sidelong glance.

"I'm fairly certain that old demon Ilias sent someone after my sisters. There was a bounty hunter at the speakeasy the other night, and I know it wasn't one of yours."

"And how do you know that?"

She flashed him a smile, all teeth. "Yours die faster," she said.

Jack scoffed. "I've never sent a bounty hunter after you, Elisabeth. Certainly not now."

"Then either Aguillard is getting bold, or his people are. I thought you were keeping him in check?"

Jack paused, turning to look at her. "This grudge against Aguillard is getting you nowhere," he reminded her, and her dark eyes narrowed. "Your little turf war's got to stop, Elisabeth. He isn't as harmless as you think he is, and if you keep pushing him——"

"Funny you'd call it a turf war," Elisabeth said. "You're the one trying to win over the new Caretaker, aren't you?"

"Aren't *you*?" he countered.

Elisabeth shrugged, gesturing for Jack to keep walking. "She's interesting," she said, her tone a little too sharply edged to be as innocent as she intended. "Gen thinks she's nothing, unsurprisingly, but I've got a hunch. This one isn't like the last one," she mused, "and if that's the case——"

"Don't touch her," Jack warned, and Elisabeth shot him an impatient glance from below the mirrored surface of her lenses.

"Please, Jack. You think I'd waste her on a meal? I have more insatiable appetites."

Jack said nothing, feeling Elisabeth's eyes trace his profile.

"Ah, I see. You want her for yourself," Elisabeth murmured, and Jack tossed her a careless look of disagreement.

"What I want has nothing to do with it. She has a job to do, and I'm teaching h-"

"Oh, of course," Elisabeth said with a mean-spirited laugh. "*Teaching* her. Is that what you usually call it?"

"You obviously warned her against me," he noted in lieu of a reply; he hardly needed to provoke her, which refuting her would unhelpfully do. "Not very sportsmanlike, Elisabeth."

"Well, I have my own interests," Elisabeth reminded him, "and anyway, she's better off not trusting you. If I could have saved her from meeting you to begin with, I'd be sainted for my efforts."

"Says the unholy creature of the night," muttered Jack.

"How long are you going to live, Jack, before you learn not to cross me?" Elisabeth lamented with a sigh, ambivalent as only she could be. "I seem to have taught you that lesson more than a few times, and yet here we are again—"

"This isn't about you or me," Jack said. "But Elisabeth, your vendettas have got to stop. Piss him off long enough and Aguillard will come for you, and when he does—"

"Aguillard isn't half the vamp I am."

"He's not what you think he is *at all*," Jack said, frustrated. "Why can't you just listen to me, Elisabeth, for once? We've had our differences, fine, but I'm not coming for you, and unless you give Aguillard a reason, he won't, either."

"I don't really play defense, Jack. I find it dull." Theatrically, she proved it with a glance at her cuticles. "Better to be rid of my threats outright."

"Just—" Jack gritted his teeth. "Look, just don't, okay? *Don't*," he repeated, hoping to sway her with sincerity, "because believe me, I don't need a reason for this stalemate between us to break."

Elisabeth considered him a moment, pausing him with a hand on his arm just before they stopped outside his tailor. She glanced at their reflection in the shop's window, which presently contained only him, and then back at his face.

"What is it about Marisa?" she asked him.

"Nothing out of the ordinary. She's the new Caretaker, that's all."

Elisabeth gave him a long look, searching him for something.

"You know, you were always most handsome when you were lying," she murmured, red lips fitting snugly over the prongs of her too-white teeth, and in answer to the little shiver she had given him, he pulled firmly from her reach.

"Leave Aguillard alone," Jack warned. "That means Ilias, too. And don't come for Marisa either, Elisabeth, because if you do—"

"Oh, save the threats, Jack," Elisabeth said, the runes of night flashing briefly in the sun from her ring. "I've stayed alive this long without any help from you. I certainly don't need it now."

Then, in a little flicker of daylight, she was gone, and he was alone, and it seemed it was finally time to buy a new suit.

It was pretty obvious to Marisa that, despite his insistence to the contrary, whether Jack St. Germaine was more or less trustworthy than Elisabeth Clavier was largely a matter of opinion.

On the one hand, it was clear Jack was influential enough that making an enemy of him was unwise; he was at least knowledgeable enough that he was helpful in some basic, logistical way. He answered her questions about her grandmother's house, and about her role, which was nothing Elisabeth had been especially interested in helping with.

On the other, it didn't take a genius to know fewer questions were being answered than not.

The next day, Marisa waited until there was no sign of Jack before slipping out to make her way back to the vampire speakeasy. She felt an indefinable sense of thrill that increasingly mixed, the further she walked, with little pearls of fear, manifesting as beads of sweat from the humid Louisiana air. Her t-shirt clung to her spine as she made her way up the steps, frowning down at the cats who seemed to be watching her just a tad too closely.

She skipped the absinthe this time, ordering a beer she'd never heard of and hoping it wasn't something she'd soon come to regret.

"Don't worry," said a voice behind her, and Marisa jumped, both startled and unsurprised to find that Elisabeth was standing behind her. She was dressed this time in an A-line black dress, which she'd worn over sheer black tights and a pair of laced-up patent leather ankle boots. Her hair was up in a French twist, a slim silver barrette holding it in place. "Just a beer," Elisabeth clarified, glancing lazily around the room, "not any kind of magical poison."

Marisa blinked. "Did you just—"

"Read your mind? Nope," Elisabeth said, taking a sip of her drink. Her white teeth bit around the narrow straw as she smiled, morbidly amused. "Which isn't to say I can't. Just that I didn't have to, and besides, it's rude." Her smile thinned. "I wouldn't."

Then she turned away, wandering elsewhere, while Marisa leapt to follow, hurrying in her wake. "Wait, Elisabeth—"

"Chasing after me, I see," Elisabeth noted without stopping, though she was walking slowly enough (strutting, Marisa would say, or perhaps sashaying) that Marisa could catch up to her. "Thought you might. Is Jack not doing it for you, then?"

She sounded amused, like it was a joke she'd tell someone else later.

"Yeah, well—about him," Marisa began uncertainly, and Elisabeth sighed, falling to a sudden halt and turning to scrutinize Marisa's look of discomfort.

"I told you not to trust him," Elisabeth reminded her. "But it's been brought to my attention that it would be unsportsmanlike for me to tell you why."

"Unsportsmanlike?"

"Yes, very," Elisabeth confirmed, and then turned her attention back to the crowd, catching the eye of a young man who winked at her from across the bar. Elisabeth smiled slowly, red lips peeling back from white teeth again, and gave him a small wave. It appeared to be a flirtation that had been going on since earlier in the night.

"Um," said Marisa, and Elisabeth beckoned the man over with a tilt of her head, the motion so subtly flirtatious Marisa was immediately flooded with envy. Elisabeth, whatever else she was, was an expert in seduction, and though Marisa wasn't entirely certain what Elisabeth intended with the man at the bar, she could see seduction was fundamentally what this was.

"Look," Marisa attempted to press her, "if you could just tell me, you know, *why* you warned me against him—"

"Well," Elisabeth cut in, flashing Marisa an exasperated glance, "if you insist on having this conversation right now—"

"I do," Marisa said staunchly.

"—then you'll have to help me with a little errand. Hi," she said to the incoming man, slipping her tongue over her lips. "Hope you don't mind me being so forward."

"Not at all," said the man, grinning. He had exceedingly moussed hair, an expensive suit, and what was surely a false tan. Marisa, who had an inkling he wasn't Elisabeth's type, wasn't sure whether to be repulsed by him or worried for his safety.

"I love strong women," he said.

Elisabeth nudged Marisa, who jumped. "That," she murmured in Marisa's ear, offering a knowing glance for conspiracy, "is code for 'I hate strong women,' so just tuck that one away. Learned that very quickly," she added, all the while continuing to smile at the man, who only seemed to become more enamored with her the more she spoke. "What's your name, darling?"

"Chad," said the man.

"Mm, what a beautiful name," Elisabeth remarked, taking Chad's hand and leading him back to the stairs. Marisa hung back, unsure what to do, until Elisabeth stopped to toss a glare over her shoulder, giving Marisa an arched brow of impatience. "Come on, then. You wanted answers, didn't you?"

It was probably a terrible idea, but unfortunately, it was also what she'd come for. Marisa hurried to follow as Elisabeth led Chad outside, making their way to a darkened corner in the back alley. Two or three cats shuffled hurriedly away, leaving nothing but undisturbed silence in their absence.

As for Chad, it seemed he either couldn't look away from Elisabeth or wouldn't. He took no notice of Marisa or where they were going, merely permitting himself to be led.

"Now, tell me," Elisabeth murmured to Chad, nudging him against the back wall of a nearby restaurant, "you were here yesterday with a young woman, weren't you?" She toyed with his tie, adding, "Pretty girl, petite, red hair. About my size?"

"Oh, sweetheart, come on now," drawled Chad, dismissing Elisabeth with a flap of his hand. "Jealousy isn't a good look. How about a smile instead?" he demurred, reaching out to curl a hand around Elisabeth's cheek.

But Elisabeth, unlike Chad, hadn't forgotten Marisa's presence. She arched a brow over her shoulder, sparing Marisa a little gesture of *I told you so* before turning back to Chad.

"What happened to her?" Elisabeth asked innocently, and Chad shrugged.

"She wasn't you, sweetheart," he said, adding smoothly, "Believe me, there hasn't been anyone like you before."

To that, Elisabeth's smile turned cold with something that gave Marisa an irrepressible chill.

"Tell me the truth," Elisabeth said, and though her voice hadn't audibly changed, there was something in the command that hadn't been there before. Even from a distance, Marisa could somehow feel the effects of Elisabeth's will filling all the little pressure points of her body, nudging into weak spots at the back of her knees and swelling at her temples like a headache. She felt distinctly uncomfortable, unsettled and trapped, as if she couldn't push away something that had closed too tightly around her airways.

It was obvious that Chad, too, was suffering a heightened degree of Marisa's symptoms. He seemed to fight it for a moment, grimacing, before grounding out, "I fucked her and didn't call. It was just sex."

"And me?" Elisabeth asked, batting her lashes.

"You're just sex, too," slid through Chad's teeth, though he looked a little disarmed at having said it.

"Mm," Elisabeth said, leaning towards him, "right. And tell me, Chad—did you even bother to make sure your guest from last night actually finished?"

By now, Chad was aware something wasn't right. The entrancement he must have felt at first—Elisabeth's natural charm, mixed with something else she possessed; looks, or something deceptively boiled down to charisma—must have been appealing enough before, but this clearly wasn't.

He looked with panic at Marisa, blinking, before his jaw wrenched open for a single word: "No."

Elisabeth's dark lips twitched, then stilled.

"I thought not," she murmured, and then Chad's pulse really began to race, evidence of it visible where his veins pulsed at his neck. A troubling sight, Marisa thought uncomfortably, particularly when Elisabeth's dark eyes fell to his throbbing carotid, her thumb tracing smoothly over the evidence of blood.

"Wait," Marisa said, and Elisabeth turned to look at her, irritated. "About Jack."

"Can't this wait?" Elisabeth asked, her hand tightening momentarily around Chad's throat until he choked, wheezing in a mix of fear and opposition. "I told you," she murmured to Marisa, "I have a little errand to run."

"I see that, but I'd kind of rather you didn't kill him," Marisa said uncertainly, as Elisabeth rolled her eyes.

"Your opposition's been noted," she said, and then sighed in apparent concession, releasing Chad with a clipped command of, "Sit."

Obediently, Chad sat, his legs collapsing under him.

"Stay," Elisabeth said coolly, and he glared at her, mutinous, but obliged as she turned back to Marisa, folding her arms over her chest. "You have five minutes," Elisabeth said flippantly, "so ask."

Seeing as that was probably the best offer Marisa was going to get, she didn't hesitate.

"Who is Jack?"

"A liar," Elisabeth said. "Next question."

"What do you mean?"

"I mean he lies, *and* he's a thief. Everything about him is stolen," Elisabeth said with a scoff, "his name included."

"Well," Marisa considered, frowning. "He *says* he's an alchemist, so—"

"He is," Elisabeth said, "among other things. Liar," she repeated, ticking them off on her fingers, "demon killer, vampire killer, regular killer—"

"Who did he," Marisa began, and winced. "How did he, um. *Why*, I guess, did he—"

"It's really not my story to tell," Elisabeth sighed with an element of annoyance, "and anyway, he's gone soft in recent years. As far as I know, Jack hasn't killed anyone or anything in almost a century, though that's at least partially my doing." She glanced down at Chad, giving him a wink, and then turned back to Marisa. "If you're worried about him hurting you, he probably won't," she said with a shrug. "He'll just trick you into something, or trap you. He's clever that way."

"Are you two..." Surely there wasn't a word for it. "Friends?"

"No," Elisabeth said, and then, "Two more questions."

"Well, you made a point of warning me against him," Marisa reminded her with a frown, "so I guess I just want to understand. If I'm in danger, or if he's..." She hesitated. "I just want to know if I can trust him, I suppose."

"Well, you can't," Elisabeth said tartly, "but obviously, you're going to. The unfortunate thing about Jack is that he does know a lot," she grudgingly permitted. She gestured to one of her many eccentric rings, adding, "He made this, for one thing, so he can be very useful to you, provided you set some boundaries. He's very powerful, very skilled, and he can answer more of your questions than I can. Just know that when he gives you an answer, he is almost certainly restricting most of the truth; be careful with relying on him. The Comte de Saint Germain was the first to pay the price for trusting Jack," Elisabeth warned, "and I highly doubt you'll be the last."

"But—" Marisa frowned. "But I thought Jack *was* the Comte."

"He is," Elisabeth said.

"But—"

"He is *now*," Elisabeth corrected impatiently. "The man born to the title of Comte and the one who eventually went down in history are two different men. One of them is wealthy and talented, skilled and learned, and in possession of a valuable secret," she said with a low laugh, "and the other, as I mentioned, is a liar. Though, a very handsome one," she conceded, grinning down at Chad, who gave her another murderous look of displeasure. "And beautiful people will ruin your life, won't they, Chad?"

Marisa could see she was losing Elisabeth's attention. "Okay, sure, but—hang on," she recalled, swallowing. "When you say he's a killer, do you mean—"

"Hey Chad," Elisabeth said, withdrawing the silver barrette from her hair and sliding a piece of it away, revealing it to have been a slim stiletto knife. "Hold this, would you?"

Chad struggled not to raise his hand, but it was a matter of seconds—blinks—before he gradually gave in, his fingers shakily unfurling. Even Marisa, subject to Elisabeth's abilities purely by proximity, had to fight from lifting her hand and accepting the knife herself as Chad's palm extended for Elisabeth's perusal.

"Thanks," Elisabeth said, smacking the stiletto into his hand. "Be careful," she advised with a laugh, and Marisa watched Chad's eyes widen as his own hand raised the knife, ostensibly without his permission, to his throat. "That's a good boy," Elisabeth murmured. "Just hold it there, love."

"Elisabeth," Marisa cut in, swallowing. "Look, I just... I *want* to believe you, but—"

"He's a lost cause, you know," Elisabeth remarked thoughtfully, and Marisa blinked.

"Who, Jack?"

"No, Chad. Focus," Elisabeth snapped, and in response, Marisa felt her brain rattle a little inside her head. "Chad's never going to learn. He's a lost cause," she sighed, bending down to look him in the eye, "along with every other man like him. Aren't you?" she said softly, and as Chad swallowed, the blade he held to his throat drew a thin, shallow line, no deeper than a papercut.

Briefly, Elisabeth smiled.

Then she leaned forward, slipping her tongue along the tiny beads of crimson, and Chad shuddered violently, lurching away from her touch.

"What's wrong, baby?" Elisabeth asked him, adopting a delicate tone of hurt. "Don't you like that?"

"Elisabeth," Marisa said hoarsely, but Elisabeth's lips were on Chad's throat again.

"Up to you," Elisabeth said to Chad's neck, her teeth grazing lightly over his skin in a motion so sensual that even Marisa shuddered with inadvisable longing. "If I bite you," Elisabeth murmured, "it'll take longer. I haven't had a proper meal in some time, and believe me, darling, I'm starving."

Elisabeth's tongue slipped out over the lobe of Chad's ear, and he forced his eyes shut.

"See her?" Elisabeth asked, wrenching his jaw with one hand to force his attention to Marisa. "She's pretty, isn't she? Look at those long legs; look at that skin, those eyes. Tempting, isn't she?"

Chad said nothing.

"Oh, you and I see similar things when we look at her, I'm sure," Elisabeth mused, "but I see something

73

you don't. I see something even she doesn't see, but Jack surely does. Because Jack's not an idiot, is he? Even if he's hardly better than you."

Marisa inhaled sharply, unsure what to do with that information.

Then, without warning, Elisabeth jerked Chad's face back towards her own, one hand clawed around his jaw.

"Me or the knife," she said, voice cold again, and Chad's breath quickened. "Your choice."

Marisa was fairly certain she should run, particularly because Chad couldn't (and what would happen when Elisabeth was done?), but there was something darkly enchanting about Elisabeth's silken voice. She was crouched in the darkened alley over a helpless man, her dress trailing on the sodden ground, and still, Marisa couldn't look away.

"Go ahead," Elisabeth said, coaxing Chad with a dangerous quiet. "Tell me, darling. How do you want your death?"

Chad struggled, glaring at her for a long moment, but having been granted permission to speak, his lips eventually parted.

"Fuck you, bitch," he spat, and in a startling motion, he slit his own throat, the blood rushing from his carotid to dribble down his tie before he immediately slumped down, limp, and gargled up the last of his air.

Marisa turned away, sickened, and heard Elisabeth rise to her feet.

"They always say that," Elisabeth lamented, shaking her head. "Men, honestly. Anyway, was that all?" she asked Marisa, who immediately took a step backwards, stumbling in retreat.

"Aren't you," Marisa attempted, struggling not to vomit or cry. "Aren't you going… to eat him, or like—" She winced, tasting bile. "Drink his blood, or—?"

"Nah," Elisabeth said, shrugging. "This?" she prompted, kicking at Chad's lifeless foot, and Marisa flinched again. "Your body's a temple, Marisa," she advised, tossing her hair over one shoulder and turning in the opposite direction. "Don't fill it with toxic shit."

When Jack arrived back at the Caretaker's house later that evening, he noted Marisa was sitting in the kitchen, staring aimlessly at the refrigerator.

"What are you looking at?" he asked her, and she glanced up, her attention traveling a long way to land on him.

She appeared to have been awake for some time, her hair pulled back into a wild, thickly-gathered ponytail with a pair of oversized glasses on her unadorned face. He supposed that was no surprise; after all, who could sleep when her only job was to be at home and open doors for monsters? He inspected her for a moment, wondering what it was about her he found so intriguing. Even compared to the countless (yes, unfortunately, he had actually lost count) liaisons he'd had in his younger days, she was something... different.

She did have a resemblance to Oscalia, who had been similarly dark-skinned and thin, but there was something to Marisa that remained unlocked, or perhaps unbroken.

"There's no wiring on the fridge," she said.

He wondered if maybe it was her cynicism that was so noticeable, then discarded it. That was hardly the core of her, and if anything, she was more analytical than cynical.

"No," he agreed. "It's not that kind of energy."

He wandered over to the fridge in question, withdrawing ingredients. "Hungry?" he asked over his shoulder, glancing up at her. She looked amused.

"I suppose an alchemist would make a good cook," she said, "so yes."

He withdrew the materials for coq au vin, which Marisa would probably not be aware was nothing more than peasant food. Jack always found it soothing, and fitting to his personal history, which was something he typically suffered relapses of whenever he spoke to Elisabeth. She had a way of reminding him about his past that was namelessly unpleasant; at least, until it could be properly stewed.

"Is something wrong?" Marisa asked him, and Jack shook his head, conjuring a bottle of brandy and sniffing its contents.

"Just ancient history," Jack said, and Marisa hesitated, but after a glance of prodding from him, she conceded to ask.

"Is it," she said, and ventured carefully, "Elisabeth?"

It was the inevitable question. He had been certain Elisabeth wouldn't leave Marisa alone despite his warning, and the prospect of her winning Marisa's trust over his was far more dangerous than the inconvenience of a few personal confessions. He set down the brandy in favor of picking up the Bordeaux, indulging a long, careful sip.

"When I say I knew Elisabeth," he clarified, setting the bottle on the counter, "I mean that she and I have a history." He cleared his throat, adding, "A romantic one."

Marisa waited, appearing to have already guessed as much, and Jack sighed.

"We fell in love in France, before she was sent to Louisiana. I had nothing," he admitted. "No money, no education… no means to have either or both. I vowed to make a life for myself, for us, and I promised to find her—which is how I came to meet the real Comte de Saint Germain. But," he exhaled, "by the time I was able to get out from under the Comte's control to find her, there was nothing left of my Elisabeth to return to. She was a monster, already bitten and angry at the world, and I barely escaped with my life. She's the one who had me exiled," he said bitterly, "and if not for Aguillard—"

"Who's Aguillard?" Marisa asked, frowning, and Jack waved a hand.

"Not important. A vampire, though not one like Elisabeth. He owns the bar," he explained, "and he has some degree of influence, but not much. Because of Elisabeth and her sisters, most of the city's creatures are in hiding. Hence the need for you," he reminded her, and she frowned.

Then she softened, or perhaps he only imagined she did. "Elisabeth betrayed you?"

"Yes," Jack said. "And not just me. In fact, Elisabeth was the reason I—"

But Marisa leapt to her feet, suddenly panicked.

"What was that?" she asked, and Jack frowned.

"What was what?"

"That… that *rumble*," she said, sounding agitated. "Didn't you feel it?"

In answer, it was difficult to remain calm. This, the inevitable result of her acceptance of the house, was starting much earlier than he'd expected, even with his inexplicable sense that Marisa was somehow different from her grandmother. Oscalia had gone some years with her husband and son before it had become something she could no longer control.

"No," Jack said, stirring idly at the stew. "A… rumble, you said?"

"Yes," Marisa said, and blinked. "It feels like—like seeing something," she said with a frown, "or… *touching* it? I know that doesn't make sense," she growled with impatience, "but it's like a sense that I didn't have before, or that doesn't belong to me, and—"

She jumped, whipping around. "Did you hear that?"

There was a loud knock at the door.

"I heard *that*," Jack informed her, but Marisa was already moving, rushing to the courtyard entrance. "Marisa, wait—"

She yanked the door open, whatever uncomfortable thing buzzing in her limbs prompting her to too-hasty action, and there, in the frame, was the demon Ilias, wearing his usual shape as an elderly man. Unlike usual, though, Ilias seemed fuzzy around the edges, the illusion wearing thin, and there was a glow of molten heat around him that set Jack's teeth on edge. It was a toxicity he'd seen before, over a century ago, and he didn't like that he was seeing it again now.

"Marisa," Jack warned, catching up to her and taking her arm. "Don't touch him—"

"I have a message for the Caretaker," said Ilias, his voice gravelly and deep.

"That's me," Marisa said, her back rigid against Jack's chest. "What's the message?"

Ilias turned his vacant stare on her, tilting his luminescent head.

"You will have a choice, Caretaker," Ilias said. "Death by your own hand, or by the creatures you will have wronged before the moon is up. If you do not claim your life yourself, then we will claim it for you."

Marisa's face went stiff. "Bullshit," she said, and then, "Who sent you?"

"Marisa," Jack warned, "don't push him. He's been tampered with, and now he's—"

"You will know soon enough," Ilias said, and then, without warning, he reached for Marisa's throat, an oppressive brightness filling the house as Marisa let out a scream, clawing for what must have been the burning around her neck.

Jack gritted his teeth, reaching behind him for the knife he'd learned to keep there since the last time he'd encountered something that couldn't be killed. It was something he had once asked the Comte, the man who had first been an alchemist: *How does one defeat a monster?*

Imbue it with humanity, the Comte had said: *with vice and virtue both*. With greed and charity. With patience and wrath, with envy and kindness. With blood, with sacrifice. With everything it took to make a human, and then with everything it took to end one, too.

It was a concoction that was slightly more difficult a stew than coq a vin, which was why Jack never lost track of the knife.

He tore it free from its scabbard and stabbed it quickly into the side of Ilias' neck, watching him warp in and out of his human form. The constraints of his disguise became less and less potent, the demon tearing free from his shell, and then Jack shoved himself between Ilias and Marisa, holding her at a distance.

"Who sent you?" he shouted at Ilias, wrenching the knife in deeper, and Ilias flickered in and out of sight. His human mouth gave a scream before becoming a vacant chasm, out of which only one thing could be heard:

"Elisabeth Clavier."

And then, with the last of Ilias' remaining ability, he let out a howl that scraped the inside of Jack and Marisa's ears, blinding them both with the final blows of his destruction.

LA PETITE MORT

PART III: The Casket Girl

Genevieve was waiting for Elisabeth in the living room; arms crossed, braless, and looking as if she'd been doing nothing but watching Netflix all evening.

Not that the inauspicious details of her appearance prevented her from sounding like a disapproving mother hen. "Did you handle the demon?"

"Yes, Gen, obviously," Elisabeth said impatiently, kicking off her ankle boots and falling into the sofa. The trouble with having so many roommates, if she could even call them that, was the impossibility of getting any peace and quiet. "What are you doing up?"

"Lou's writing." They'd all managed to do something productive with their eternally undead lives; Louisa was a romance writer, Genevieve was a tour guide, and Elisabeth was... making the best of her talents. The important thing was that Louisa had finally lived long enough to stop using a male pseudonym, which meant her business was now reliant only on her ability to produce a new book every two months. Her primary demonic capacity was the speed of her typing. "And Jeanie's not back yet."

"She's not?" Elisabeth asked, surprised. "I told her to stay local tonight."

Genevieve shrugged. "Hence me asking about the demon. I thought maybe you'd had some trouble and needed help."

"Please, Gen." Help was the one thing Elisabeth had never needed. Not since she'd left Jack (*Jacques*, at the time) in France. Though, maybe if she'd excised him from her life sooner, she'd have done a lot more much faster—and *without* having to board a disease-ridden ship first.

Granted, if that had been the case, Lou would hardly have as much fodder for her books. Elisabeth's farce of a love story was a favorite of hers; the poetic little goblin. Luckily, Elisabeth was a believer in being the sum of her experiences, so she didn't fault Jack for his most recent crimes (i.e., the attempted robbery of her life, or maybe her will). He couldn't have known what she would become; neither had she. All the better for both of them that he had failed her in the end.

At least she'd chosen well; she had loved a man who managed to make something of himself eventually, for all that he was a blip of error in her origin story. She'd been right to see some spark of value in him, even if it wasn't the one she'd initially thought.

"Well, I can't imagine you killed him," said Genevieve, stirring Elisabeth from her thoughts.

"Who, Ilias? Of course not." Killing demons was beyond even a vampire's capacity for violence. It involved killing much more than a body, and vampirism was deeply corporeal. Kill a mortal body, you typically killed its mind, too. There wasn't exactly a shortcut to closing down a void of ancient knowledge, or whatever Ilias was supposed to be.

Elisabeth had only known one person to pull it off, and the demon he'd killed, while infamous, had been relatively young. "That would be like poisoning the well of an oracle."

"Still, Ilias is crossing lines. Hasn't before. Unusual," Genevieve murmured, "don't you think?"

Genevieve had a tendency for skepticism. Unfortunately, she was also a little psychic. No telling how related those things were, or what it said about the world that the most cynical of all of them was usually right. "Something you'd like to say, Gen?"

"Nothing. Just a feeling, that's all."

"Mortals feel. *We* have instincts, and trained ones." Elisabeth rose to her feet, pausing just south of Genevieve's gaze; barefoot, she was smaller than almost all her sisters. Tricky things, appearances. "If you think there's a problem, Gen, let's fix it."

Genevieve slid her a listless glance. "Thought you were distracted."

"Distracted?"

A shrug. "Jack. The Caretaker. Either one." Another shrug. "Both."

Ah. So it was this again. "Marisa's useful, Gen, or at least she could be. On our side," Elisabeth clarified, "she's useful."

"Your side, you mean."

Hadn't Elisabeth proven often enough those were one and the same? She drummed her fingers against her thigh, impatient. "If something is bothering you, Genevieve, perhaps you ought to just tell me."

"She's living with Jack, Elisabeth, and she reads *romance novels*, for fuck's sake. She's just a mortal looking for someone to rescue her, and you and I both know that's Jack's specialty. After all, he tricked you," Genevieve pointed out, "didn't he? Just like all those other women."

"Please. He didn't *trick* me." An irritating mostly-truth.

"Ah, my mistake. So you didn't love him, then?"

The best thing about Genevieve (and inconveniently, also the worst) was her complete incapability to soften a point.

"If I did, it certainly wasn't because he tricked me. It was because I had no better options." Elisabeth gave Genevieve a little glare, resuming the argument they'd already had enough times to fill whatever remained of their eternity. "When I knew him, Jack was a clever nobody with a silver tongue, and I was an orphan destined to die in childbirth like my mother. Now I know better."

"But the Caretaker doesn't."

"She will," Elisabeth said firmly. "I'll make sure of it. She listens to me," she added, "I can tell. She came looking for me tonight."

That prompted half a laugh out of Genevieve. "She did? Well," she exhaled, rolling her eyes, "no wonder you sent Jeanie off on her own, then."

Elisabeth bristled. "What's that supposed to mean?"

"Nothing."

"Gen," Elisabeth growled, "do you really think I put Jeanie in danger? She's two centuries old. I think she can handle herself."

"Of course she can."

"Then what are you—"

"I'm just saying, it's not the Caretaker's *power* you want," Genevieve informed her smartly, "it's the Caretaker herself."

Slowly, Elisabeth permitted a scowl.

"What possible interest would I have in a mortal?"

"Oh," Genevieve scoffed, "so now she's just a mortal?"

"She's a mortal until she's not," Elisabeth said, "and at this rate, she won't be anything. Certainly not if Jack's with her." He had a way of keeping people to a certain level of muted satisfaction; stifling them, subduing them, to the point of near captivity. He'd once managed to convince Elisabeth that undying love and a cottage in the country would be enough to satisfy them both, and look at them now.

She wondered, as she often did, if he'd known it was a lie even then.

"Are you jealous of Marisa?" she asked Genevieve, shaking herself of the thought. "It's not as if my priorities have changed."

"Marisa I can take or leave," Genevieve replied, impassive. "I'm just wondering when you'll notice that this, like everything in your life, is about Jack."

"That's ridiculous."

"Is it? Because it seems to me you only want her because Jack wants her," Genevieve commented, at which point Elisabeth grew impatient with her speculation.

"Gen, all of this is really very simple. Ilias spilled blood on our side of the city. We spoke, we resolved it, end of story. Marisa is the meridian now, and so long as she controls the pitch, we're under her jurisdiction. Or do you want another Oscalia keeping us at bay?"

"I'm just saying, Lise—"

"Elisabeth," came a solemn voice behind them. Elisabeth and Genevieve both turned in unison to find Jeanie in the doorway, flanked by an equally somber Denise and Marie. "We have a problem."

Elisabeth flashed Genevieve a quieting glance, warning her they'd finish their discussion later.

"What is it?"

"Ilias attacked the new Caretaker," Jeanie said, and Elisabeth blinked, surprised. "He came for her less than an hour ago, threatening her life."

"That's ridiculous. Ilias is entirely out of line." Something was wrong with the demon, clearly. He knew better than to stir up trouble like that.

"It gets worse." Jeanie's lips were pressed to a thin line. "I heard Aguillard's people discussing it outside their speakeasy—"

"That's unusual for Aguillard." Elisabeth's eyes narrowed, immediately suspicious. "I've never known him to let his people speak freely about much of anything."

"We heard rumors, too," Denise cut in, referencing herself and Marie. "It's everywhere."

"And it's bad," Marie confirmed, while Elisabeth fought the need to roll her eyes.

'Bad' was an overrated ruling, in her mind. Having been through plenty of it before, her scale for gauging disaster was rather different from most. 'Bad,' for Elisabeth, was being transported to Louisiana from France as orphans without protection; without a single possession but a casquette chest; without the option of saying no. 'Bad' was watching half the others die on the crossing alone, their bodies tossed into the ocean before the smell could rot the air. 'Bad' was arriving here with the promise of freedom only to be groped, grabbed, and assaulted; to be taken hostage by a city full of desperate, disgusting, poverty-stricken men. 'Bad' was learning to either inflict pain or take it, because it could only be one or the other. 'Bad' was knowing a violation would have to be made, and it would either be him or be you.

'Bad' was the stranger she took for the normal kind of violent until he transformed into something beyond even the scope of her nightmares. 'Bad' was finding out the New World was even more savage than she thought. 'Bad' was struggling to see through bleary eyes the blood on her hands from the sisters she tried to save and couldn't. 'Bad' was watching them survive an ocean of disease only to die anyway, punctures gaping from their lifeless necks because they couldn't take the things she could. 'Bad' was being one of only twelve when there had once been hundreds, huddled together on a single mattress beside the sea of empty beds.

'Bad' was aging while failing to age, thinking her lover dead and mourning him for decades, only to learn he had spent a century lavishing himself in wealth and women, foregoing his promise to her and forgetting his devotion entirely. 'Bad' was him betraying her. 'Bad' was him deciding the world was no longer big enough for the both of them; that only one of them could survive. 'Bad' was knowing how sweetly he could kiss her, while seeing just how bitterly the whole thing was a lie.

Elisabeth Clavier had known bad a thousand times over. Certainly enough times to recognize it without fear.

"Out with it," she said.

"They're saying Ilias delivered a warning to the new Caretaker," Jeanie explained to Elisabeth. "That you sent him after her to kill her."

"Ridiculous," Elisabeth scoffed. "Why would anyone believe that?"

"They have no choice but to believe it, because Ilias is dead. Murdered."

Genevieve frowned. "By whom?"

They all turned slowly to Elisabeth, who hardly needed to hear his name to know precisely who had done it.

"Oh," she said, grimacing.

So then this was bad, too.

On some practical level, Marisa understood she was most likely in shock. *A demon tried to kill me*, she thought numbly. *A vampire sent a demon after me to try to kill me, and now he's dead.*

He's dead, she thought again, and the message right before he'd been killed had been: *You will be soon.*

"Drink this," Jack said, shoving something into her hand. He'd rushed out the moment the demon had been dispatched, but immediately upon his return he'd busied himself around the house, boiling something (or brewing it, who knew) on the stove before pouring it into a pleasantly innocuous ceramic mug.

"Marisa?"

She heard him through a fog, hesitantly closing her fingers around the cup. The last thing she wanted was to eat or drink; even breathing was a chore. She seemed to hitch at every peak and valley, artless and out of practice. Inhale, pause at full; exhale, pause at empty.

Why was this so bad? Was it because it was so incomprehensible? She wanted to call her sister. She wanted her mother. She wanted the security of her past. She wanted everything but what she was: alone in New Orleans. Alone in a strange house with nothing. Alone, except for demons and the haunting stink of death.

"Drink it," Jack said again, and then his palm was curled around her cheek, lifting the cup to her lips on her behalf. It smelled like cinnamon, maybe a little nutmeg, and at the end of a long breath, Marisa thought she inhaled a touch of sanity, which smelled suspiciously like lemongrass. "Slowly," he assured her, and she forewent a nod in favor of taking a sip, letting the liquid settle on her tongue before it made its way down her throat.

It took two sips to emerge from the fog, and then two more for her thoughts to feel close to lucid. They settled from where they'd danced in agitation, gradually resolving themselves to recognition of a single, unassailable detail of the night.

"Elisabeth," she realized aloud, and Jack looked somber.

"I warned you about her."

"I know." Marisa closed her eyes, exhaling, as little pricks of her memory returned, like the painful awakening of a sleeping limb. "It's her M.O., isn't it?"

Kill yourself or I'll kill you. That had been the message earlier that evening from Ilias, an echo of what Marisa had seen when Elisabeth presented death to Chad. The image of him slitting his own over-tanned throat prompted a renewed shudder, fracturing Marisa's thoughts in silence, and Jack's hand smoothed over her cheek again, tucking itself in the base of her ponytail. An intimate place for his touch to be, but she was grateful for it. She felt grounded; anchored.

"She does love the particular masochism of choice," Jack said grimly. "Free will is one of Elisabeth's favorite weapons."

"Why?"

Jack shrugged. "I don't pretend to understand her. Elisabeth is a bit of a sadist."

"Of course she is," Marisa muttered. "She's a vampire."

"That's secondary," he assured her, and it was almost funny. For a second, Marisa almost laughed. The tea was relaxing, soothing, and Jack's touch was warm.

"You saved my life," she noted, and he gave her a long, inexpressive look.

"Should I have let you die?"

"No, I just meant..." She trailed off. "I don't know what I meant."

His eyes were bright with concern, the blue in them crisply saturated. He seemed to be surveying her for something, though she couldn't imagine what. She leaned into his hand, brushing her cheek against the inside of his wrist, and his fingers tightened in her hair.

She turned to slide her lips against his forearm, resting the mug in her lap.

"Will you let her kill me?" she asked, and he swallowed.

"No." A pause. "I won't let anything happen to you, I promise."

She could feel his pulse beside her ear; how very *alive* he was. She thought of Elisabeth's voice and the palpability of her yearning. Elisabeth was so cold, so unnaturally still, so brutally immovable. Elisabeth was dead; *undead*, and that was worse. She was a trick of the light, a little mutation of circumstance, but Jack was real, tangible, solid.

Beneath Marisa's feet, the ground rumbled its approval of her thoughts.

She could feel Jack's proximity like a hearth, like a flame. She looked up at him, eyeing the auburn curl of distress that had tumbled onto his forehead.

"Do you have to be somewhere?" she asked him.

He shook his head slowly.

"Good. Don't." She slid her hand over his. "Don't make me sleep alone tonight, Jack. I won't be able to."

He swallowed. She recalled the motion on Chad, and the way Elisabeth had slid her tongue over the pearlescent drops of blood there. Elisabeth was inhuman. Death would be nothing to her, just like life was nothing to her. Sex was probably less than nothing.

Marisa thought of Elisabeth and shivered, imagining her porcelain skin. It would be lifeless against white sheets, almost ghostly. Unwrapped, what would Elisabeth be? Smaller without her armor, without her weapons. She would still have that meanness, though; that bite. Those *bites*. Marisa pictured Elisabeth's lips sliding back from her teeth and pulled Jack closer, one of her hands curling around the back of his neck.

"Marisa," he said in her ear. A cautioning sound.

He smelled earthy, like a rustle of leaves. Whatever he'd brewed for her, she could feel the way it had come from the earth, crawling through her limbs and tightening around her chest, tangling up like vines. "What did you give me?"

"Just something to calm your nerves. To settle your thoughts."

How accommodating of him, the maybe-lying witch. It wasn't like being drunk, wanting him like this. There was no drowsiness of intoxication, only clarity, and nothing about this felt new. She'd catalogued glimpses of this feeling when she'd met him—spots of longing that changed color, floating and sizzling, like looking at a too-bright light—but it was overwhelmingly clear now. Static fell away, and it was obvious. He was standing between her legs and she was aligning her torso with his, cat-like, and it was nice that he was so tall. He had a pleasant broadness. Earlier that night, Marisa had felt Elisabeth Clavier's voice slide behind her eyes, reaching into her mind and tapping at her thoughts, and now Jack had saved her life. He was an anchor, keeping her from drifting out to sea.

He's a liar, said Elisabeth, and Marisa thought, *Yeah? So are you.*

"Jack," she said, and looked up, finding his too-bright eyes on hers. "My thoughts are plenty settled."

When he kissed her, she tasted him like sunrise, dawning warmly on her tongue.

"You can't do this," Elisabeth spat, furious, and Aguillard shrugged.

"You sent a demon after the Caretaker," he commented neutrally, "and now a respected member of our community is dead. There must be consequences— even for you, Casket Girl."

"I didn't send Ilias after anyone," Elisabeth reminded him, and Aguillard's lips twitched, half-smiling.

"Come now, you understand, don't you? I'm a concerned business owner, Mademoiselle Clavier. I must act as I see fit."

"Oh, please." The idea that his primary concern was his *business* was laughable. "You're a politician, Aguillard."

"In this case, it hardly matters. My only interest is public safety."

"Which you think you can accomplish by declaring open season on me and my sisters?" Elisabeth scoffed. "The moment this is public knowledge, they'll come for us." A blacklist was never about safety; it was as good as a burn notice, and plenty of people had cause for retaliation against them as it was.

No, Elisabeth thought grimly. Not against them. "My sisters will be collateral," she corrected herself with a grimace, "when they inevitably come for *me*."

"Well, it's been a long time coming, no?" Aguillard prompted, endlessly entertained by her misfortune. "You have many more enemies than friends."

She glared at him. "You've killed just as many mortals as I have, Aguillard."

"Mm, but I have such a sparkling personality. And a better sense of boundaries."

"What's that supposed to mean?"

"Just that it wasn't me who crossed the city's lines. If you had kept to your side—"

"Ilias crossed the line, not me!"

"That," Aguillard mused, "appears to be largely a matter of opinion. After all, why should anyone not believe you sent Ilias after the Caretaker, hm? Everyone witnessed your little disagreement with him the other night."

"That," Elisabeth snapped, "was at your invitation."

"Ah, yes, well. There's always the Jack St. Germaine of it all," Aguillard reminded her. "He, as I'm sure you know, is not very pleased with your little attack on his new pet."

"It wasn't—" Elisabeth gritted her teeth, furious, but knew Aguillard would only enjoy it more if she lost her temper. He was no match for her unless she was weak, which she only was when she was angry. Impulsivity had never suited her; unlike Jack, she was better when she was calculated, and far more deadly with a plan. "It wasn't an attack," she said flatly, exhaling her agitation. "What it is, Aguillard, is a lie, and surely you know it."

"Jack says differently," Aguillard remarked, "and I'm sure you're aware that I am only capable of acting within highly limited constraints. His word goes, I'm afraid."

Elisabeth grimaced. It wasn't the first time Jack had fucked her. Too bad she hadn't actually enjoyed it for the last hundred years. One of these days, she'd finally manage to find a metaphorical strap-on and pound it right into his—

"Language," murmured Aguillard, chuckling, and Elisabeth glared at him. Of course he'd barge into the only place a vampire didn't have to be invited: her thoughts.

"Poor form," she spat. As a rule, she never invaded other people's minds.

"Do better," Aguillard advised, eyeing his fingernails. "If you leave a door open—"

Speaking of open doors. "What's to keep me from killing you right now?" she demanded, leaning forward to place her hands squarely on his desk. "If you really want to end me as a rival, Aguillard, I can certainly do the same *without* making every creature in NOLA an arrow aimed straight for you."

He leaned back in his chair, considering her. "A compelling argument. Though," he mused, "what good would killing me do, exactly?"

An idiotic first question. "Without you, I could undo the blacklist."

"It's Jack who's blacklisting you, not me," he reminded her. "I'm just enforcing it. And even if I chose not to enforce it, the task would only fall to someone else."

"Well, then I'll do it because I can. Because I would enjoy it. Or, possibly because I've had a very stressful day," she informed him, drumming her scarlet nails against his desk, "and it would really brighten my evening to drive a piece of furniture into the inconsequential deadness you call a heart."

To her immense displeasure, Aguillard's lips quirked up with amusement.

"Do you keep track of your sisters at all times, Casket Girl? Because I do," he murmured, and Elisabeth stiffened, concealing the tightening of her knuckles as she buried the tips of her nails in her palms. "And unlike you, I do not fail to make arrangements in the event my enemies try to come for me."

"Leave my sisters out of it. They shouldn't even be part of the blacklist."

"Not my orders," he repeated. "Surely you realize Jack would never be stupid enough not to include them. We all know what you would do, given free rein."

Her mouth tightened. "Jack doesn't come for them. He comes for me. This," she told him firmly, "is *your* doing."

"Maybe that was true once," Aguillard said with a shrug, "but surely he's noticed you're much better behaved when you have a little more at stake."

"My own life isn't enough to threaten?" she demanded, incensed.

"Not if he wants you neutralized," Aguillard replied, "which, I assure you, he does."

"You mean you do."

His smile thinned. "Whatever helps you sleep at night, Mademoiselle Clavier," he murmured, and while she was certain it was intended to taunt her, or perhaps even to confuse her, she fell unwillingly into his trap of wondering whose motives to trust.

"Jack needs to put a tighter leash on you," she said, turning to leave, but paused at the sound of Aguillard's low laugh, feeling it quake in the notches of her rigid spine.

"Funny," remarked Aguillard. "I was just thinking the very same thing."

Marisa's head rested indolently on Jack's chest when she whispered, tentatively, "Is it true you killed a demon before?"

Jack hated that there was only one way she could have known that. It brought him back to another moment long ago; to another bed, another time... another pillow talk confession.

Another woman, soft and pliant for a rare moment of intimacy, lying tranquilly in his arms.

How did you do it? Kill a demon. I tried and failed at least twice.

I'm surprised you lived long enough to try a second time.

Well, she was cruel, not smart. And she didn't think of me as a threat.

Then you can see how easily I killed her, Lise. She was obviously much too stupid to live.

He blinked away the image of Elisabeth's dark eyes, trading them for the amber of Marisa's. She had one leg slipped between his; his hand ran mindlessly along the line of her thigh.

"Her name was Madame Blanque," he said. "Otherwise known as Delphine LaLaurie."

Marisa looked up, frowning. "The widow?"

She was common in New Orleans lore: a widowed socialite and serial killer, whose mansion on Royal Street had contained quarters of tortured and murdered slaves.

"Not human," Jack supplied in explanation, "which is probably obvious, given her crimes. She took quite a bit of pleasure in toying with mortals." A young demon, and one who was still academic about humanity, Delphine was eager to experience the richness of abject pain: the sounds it made, the look of it, the smell and taste of anguish. To a creature as young as she was, the excruciation must have been bliss. "It was Elisabeth and her sisters who eventually chased her out of the city."

"Elisabeth did?" Marisa echoed, bitterly surprised. "I thought she'd be fine with killing mortals."

"There's," Jack began, and hesitated, reluctant to admit, "There's usually a pattern to Elisabeth's behavior. It's wrong, but rarely senseless." He paused, tracing circles on Marisa's skin, before adding, "She would have found LaLaurie repugnant."

That, and Elisabeth's victims were men, almost always. Usually a certain type of man. With the exception of sending Ilias after Marisa, Jack had never seen her attack someone without evidence of something she considered a moral violation.

Marisa, however, was still asking about the demon. "And after she was run out of New Orleans, Delphine went...?"

"To Paris," he said, and Marisa blinked. "She wasn't very discreet. I came across her very quickly following her arrival."

"You killed her in France?"

He nodded. "Otherwise, she'd have done the same thing in Paris as she did in New Orleans."

"No, of course, I just meant—" Marisa broke off, frowning at something in her thoughts. "Had you already known by then that Elisabeth was alive in New Orleans?"

Jack hesitated, then shook his head. "No," he said, and kissed her forehead, coaxing her more fully into his arms. "Sleep," he advised, and though she resisted for a moment, obviously expecting more of an answer, he nudged a little persuasion into his tone. It wouldn't take much, after the evening she'd had, to convince her brain that its best option was to quietly loosen its pondering, and luckily it wouldn't cost him much, either. Within a few moments, Marisa was breathing steadily against his chest, leaving him to toy with the curls of her hair while he stared at her ceiling in silence.

What Jack hadn't told Marisa was that the death of Delphine LaLaurie had been the start of his current incarnation. It had been the demon who had used the name Elisabeth Clavier for the first time in nearly a century, twisting it around her tongue with spite after Jack had lodged his knife into her chest. He didn't mention, for obvious reasons, that the demon's blood on his hands had tangled him, however briefly, in Elisabeth's sheets again, until they had each learned the truth about what the other had become.

For a moment, the image of Marisa in his arms flickered back to Elisabeth. How peaceful Marisa was compared to her. Elisabeth was full of violence; he could feel it in her thoughts, in the way she buzzed instead of slept. It had become exceptionally clear that whatever ills she had, nothing he could offer would possibly cure them. The day Jack had woken up to find her gone had been no great surprise.

Marisa moved in her sleep, starting to dream of something or other, and Jack slid out from under her, covering her with the duvet and making his way down the stairs.

In recent years, Jack's magic had seen a decline that he had combated with upgrades in technology. Some witches found it difficult, being staunchly opposed to the non-sentience of a computer screen, but he had learned to like it; to prefer it, even. Locator spells were far more accurate with Google Maps than with a globe or an atlas. Within moments of opening his laptop on the kitchen counter, the pale glow of Elisabeth's presence hovered nearby, traveling slowly as she walked the French Quarter streets at night.

She wouldn't run, of course; she hadn't with her banishment to one side of the city, and she wouldn't with the blacklist, either. It wasn't in her nature to flee. Elisabeth, for all that she was clever and talented, had tied herself inextricably to the city, and thereby to her own ferocious past. Even with a mark against her name, she wouldn't leave.

That, and inevitably, she would come for him. For both of them.

Jack leaned against his elbows, scraping a hand over the cheeks he really needed to shave. It was hard not to think of the way Marisa's skin felt beneath his fingers, full of life and warmth and longing. He watched the glow of Elisabeth's presence pause briefly, as if she'd stopped to look at something, or to think, and then he thought of Marisa upstairs, innocent and vulnerable in her sleep.

Jack rose to his feet and snapped his fingers, turning water to espresso.

He would have to do something about
Elisabeth. Clearly, it was going to be a long night.

Elisabeth paused where she stood, registering
something troubling. Women typically had better sense
than to wander city streets at night, but she had
personally lost the powerlessness of womanhood long
ago. Creatures of the night were far more in tune with
night itself, identifying waves of disruption within the
familiarity of recognition, and she sensed it now: the not-
rightness that told her something was wrong. The air was
thick with it, stale with something foreign and misplaced.
It was marked by something that had always meant
trouble, beginning with the time she'd first heard it
coming from the other side of the Ursuline door.

Silence.

Emptiness wasn't a natural thing; especially not in a
city full of people and creatures both. Silence was a lure,
with captivity either implied or intended to follow.

Elisabeth spun, teeth bared.

"Come on, then," she gritted to the vacant dark,
rotating slowly. It was quick work, but there could be no
doubt: this was a result of her blacklist. For years, she'd

cultivated a reputation that meant no one should have dared to come for her, but all it took was one man. One man to say she no longer mattered, and all that work was undone. "It's open season, isn't it?"

She wore a knife strapped to her thigh; habit. The pin in her hair would take out an eye in less than a blink, but she doubted this was any mortal's doing. No way to tell what kind of weaponry she would need until she knew what it was she was facing.

A hand slipped over her mouth from behind her, a jab to her kidney sending a shudder of remembered pain. Luckily, memory had never killed her before, and it certainly wouldn't tonight. She spun, furious, and whatever it was disappeared and reformed, dancing at her back.

Definitely not mortal. The knife would do her no good.

"Coward," she snapped.

No answer. This time, she felt the air in her throat close off, an invisible hand wrapping itself around her neck. She fought it, tapping the strength that could snap a spinal cord clean in half just to keep her airways from closing, and whatever it was—demon, or something even less corporeal, most likely, like an enchantment—lifted her from her feet, her rapidly-cycling heels scraping over the ground as panic struck her blind and stupid, infecting all her instincts.

Fighting for her life was an old feeling; a dead one, but it resurrected easily. It was the old race of hysteria stampeding through her chest, with the old flood of bile and copper filling her mouth. It was the palate she could no sooner forget than the tastes of her youth; the rare exquisiteness of fear that was as familiar to her tongue as the childhood spices of rosemary, marjoram and lavender, or the accessibility of Jack's name.

Jack, she registered, abruptly murderous. *This is Jack's doing.*

How easily she forgot she wasn't ruled by mortal weakness anymore.

Elisabeth's fingers twitched, the life in them briefly suspended as she channeled something else; the feelings she'd never known how to name. If other vampires were not the creature she was, it was because they had never been the mortal she had been, either. Whatever it was she possessed—resilience, or just a damned refusal to die—she used it to unclench the spectral tendrils around her throat one by one, subjecting it to the contortions of her mind.

She felt the twist of anguish, the snapping of its constitution from the contours of her will. They'd made

a mistake, the men who wronged her. The forces which
conspired to belittle her, a woman born to be nothing
but a prize or a pawn, had been the tide that turned her
into what she was. Fuck the saintliness of femininity, the
divinity of womanhood. The most female thing about
her was her anger, and she used it to rip out the claws
that dug into her throat, tearing them free with a howl of
something too stubborn to be pain.

The moment her feet touched the ground, she ran.

She'd long outlasted the need to flee the things that
chased her, but sometimes it was everything, the only
thing, to run until her lungs gave out. Behind her, the
silence whipped like wind around her ears, and for miles,
every mortal would stir restlessly from sleep, subjected to
little doldrums that, in the morning, they would not
know how to name.

Aftershocks of Elisabeth Clavier's rage.

Marisa roused late, finding a note from Jack in his
absence. *Taking care of things*, he said evasively, leaving
behind coffee in the pot with poached eggs and toast on
a mysteriously (magically, she reminded herself) warmed
plate. She sat down to eat and felt a swift tug somewhere

within her chest, closing her eyes to press the heel of her hand between her lungs and then opening them again to find herself beside the guest house door.

More creatures; something Marisa was slowly, unpleasantly, growing accustomed to. Two amorphous, warping, genderless beings arrived together, followed by what looked like a six-year-old Victorian girl who made the ground shake when she spoke. Each time Marisa sat down to take another bite of breakfast, the yolk dribbling on toast, she found herself drawn back to the guest house, which was steadily increasing in occupants.

"You're welcome," she muttered to an inhumanly pale and impossibly thin man who slammed the door in her face. He, like the others, took to his quarters with the indication he didn't care to be burdened with either pleasantries or gratitude.

Marisa made her way back to the kitchen, sitting down to try for the fourth time, only to find her kitchen was occupied.

"You fucked him," remarked Elisabeth, turning from where she'd leaned against the counter to raise a brow at Marisa, "didn't you?"

She was wearing an oversized black blazer, like the first time Marisa had seen her, belted over skinny black jeans. Her hair was pulled back, left in a sleek river down her back, to reveal a thin ribbon around her neck; a rivulet of velvet against the pale column of her throat.

"That wasn't mind-reading either, by the way. This is just what he makes after sex," Elisabeth observed neutrally, gesturing to the breakfast plate.

Marisa, meanwhile, glanced around, considering where to find a weapon. There was still a pan out on the stove, but she looked up to find Elisabeth's lips pursed, disapproving. "Don't you dare *Three Stooges* this," she warned, and stepped around the kitchen island, prompting Marisa to stumble into the wall behind her.

"What are you doing here?" Marisa demanded, driven to retreat.

Elisabeth paused a foot away from Marisa, the two of them nearly eye-to-eye with the assistance of her impossibly narrow heels. "Scared?" Elisabeth asked drily, flicking her dark gaze over Marisa, who swallowed.

"No," she lied, "but in case you've forgotten, you did recently send a demon to kill me."

Elisabeth rolled her eyes. In a breath, she had Marisa pressed further against the wall, closing the space between them without even taking a step.

"If I wanted to kill you, Marisa, don't you think I would have done it already? Believe me," she mused, running the tip of her middle finger along the line of

Marisa's clavicle, "I'd want to watch the life go out of you myself." Her lips slid up with a smile, eyes still on Marisa's neck, as she offered softly, "I bet you'd die so beautifully."

It was devastating, really, how something so grotesque could sound so wistful.

Marisa struggled to breathe, forcing out, "Jack will be back soon."

"I'm sure he will." Elisabeth's eyes, when they rose to Marisa's, were precisely the opposite of Jack's. Elisabeth's were cavernous, blinding in their enormity, sparking alongside the parting of her lips. "Interesting, really," she murmured, "that after everything I said, you'd go to him."

"He," Marisa began, and stopped. "He saved my life."

She was keenly aware of Elisabeth's scent, floral and sharp; divinely, gloriously feminine, a blade of ethereality flashing in what little space remained between them.

"Lives," Elisabeth said, "are meant to be taken back, not saved."

Her thumb stroked along Marisa's jaw, forcing her chin up with brutal softness to close one hand around the base of Marisa's throat. Briefly, with a motion of perfect symmetry, an image flashed in Marisa's mind of

Elisabeth's ponytail wrapped around her knuckles, the parting of Elisabeth's painted lips producing a gasp they might have shared with equal satisfaction.

Elisabeth was speaking again, the sound of her voice permeating Marisa's merciless thoughts, her morbid imagination. How strange it was, being so close to death; looking it in the face, grasping the finery of all its features.

"If you wanted to feel closer to me, Marisa, all you had to do was ask."

The taste of it was undeniably compelling, sweetly gruesome; a promise and a threat, and an unsettling temptation. Elisabeth's fingers were making their way down Marisa's torso, pressing into her waist, and Marisa was helplessly leaned forward, her forehead against Elisabeth's to be followed by her cheek, and then her nose. It was the motion of Marisa's unsteady breath, finally, that was the last thing to collide with Elisabeth, who hung back, drawing Marisa closer without even the smallest mercy of motion; with nothing at all, at first. Marisa's lips blindly found hers, and then it was a slip of Elisabeth's cruel, beatific tongue, cool and impassive before searing through Marisa's limbs, feverish.

A scrape of teeth. The honeyed taste of luxury, the wine-red flavor of Chanel, or maybe Dior. A lungful of perfumed air. A kiss that went on for half a moment, endlessly, and lasted infinitesimally, for years. It was trauma and mortality, legend and mythology, and then, out of oblivion, a little whisper of, "Does he taste like me?"

"No," Marisa breathed before she could stop herself, and felt the twitch of Elisabeth's satisfied smile.

Then she was gone, and Marisa was left alone to stumble, graceless, into the stable disenchantment of her absence.

PART IV: The Entrepreneur

Damian Aguillard rapped three times on the old house's door, a flake of paint falling to the shiny polish of his shoes. The house was hardly in ideal shape; though, like most things, its appearance wasn't what mattered. What it contained was far more important.

The new Caretaker appeared at the door, obviously unsettled to have a visitor. He wasn't her first for the day, Aguillard assumed. He paused a moment to focus on her thoughts, which were… erratic. Ah yes, Elisabeth Clavier had been there. That explained most things, if not everything.

"Yes?" asked the girl. Marisa, Aguillard recalled.

"Is Jack in residence?" he asked, though he was fairly certain the alchemist was not. That seemed to be part of the Caretaker's rattled appearance, in fact. Her radiating sense of displeasure was deeply informative. Clearly, Jack St. Germaine had been away most of the morning.

"He's in the other room," Marisa said. "May I help you?"

Aguillard permitted a twitch of a smile, which he could see she found irritating. A marvelous difference, he thought, between Marisa and her grandmother. Where the young Marrero heir clearly possessed a coiled sense of danger that was attached to a remarkably short fuse, Oscalia Marrero had taken her fear to its opposite ideation; she'd become frightened, resigned, easily spooked. In short, exceedingly unproductive. Obstinacy was a marvelous change of pace, even if it did mean this would take longer.

"Perhaps you might invite me in," Aguillard suggested. "A cup of tea, if you have it?"

He could see Marisa calculating this. Her mental processes were very quick, for a mortal, though she apparently lacked the refinement of Southern hospitality. "I assume you're aware you can't refuse me," he pointed out, and this time, her hesitation was a result of her obvious surprise.

"You're a creature?" she asked, frowning. "Then why use the front door?"

"Because I'm not an animal," he replied, and presented her with the beginnings of an amicable handshake, opting not to mention that he had been there many times, in fact, and only taken this mode of entry to have this very conversation. He suspected most mortals became unfriendly when they learned someone had been on their property uninvited, and he did have grand plans of digging something up from her before he carried on.

"Most call me Aguillard," he offered. "I'm told you paid a visit to my establishment recently?"

She registered his name, in addition to Jack's face. "Oh, right. Aguillard."

He took that as an opportunity to invite himself inside, seeing as she was no closer to offering him entry and, strictly speaking, he had already been invited (however reluctantly) by someone else before.

The house, as far as he could tell from the doorway, had seen no obvious changes since Marisa's arrival. Traces of Jack's work hovered impetuously around, nosy and observant. Over the years, Aguillard had noticed Jack's power had a tendency to warp the wood.

"What exactly do you do?" Marisa asked, watching Aguillard inspect the banister of the staircase. This particular warp meant a protection spell; a new one, and shoddily done, which was unsurprising. The old ones were deepened into the floorboards, holding fast for having been cast by a more capable witch; or, rather, one that had been more capable at the time.

"I own a bar," Aguillard said, observing the dust patterns in the air. They seemed localized to the main house, centering around something he assumed was in the kitchen. He turned, following the tightening radius, and added over his shoulder, "I serve on the local entrepreneurship council."

Marisa followed warily. "Council?"

"Yes. Sort of a Better Business Bureau, only for creatures," he clarified, finding the central location of the particles hovering overhead. Jack's laptop was sitting out on the center of the kitchen island and Aguillard flipped it open, observing it without much optimism. Whatever Jack had been up to, he was clever enough to have deleted any evidence of it, though hopefully only superficially. Aguillard rested a hand on the keys, waiting.

"That's private," Marisa said, sounding unsure, and Aguillard looked up, observing her. She was very pretty, and starkly Elisabeth Clavier's opposite—tall and skeptical instead of diminutive and cross, and bronze instead of ivory. She wasn't entirely unlike her predecessor; the resemblance to Oscalia was certainly there, with Marisa's height and her wild hair, except that Oscalia had grown stooped and blind, becoming useless in her later life. She had rotted like bad fruit.

"How much do you know about the creatures who stay in your home?" Aguillard asked neutrally, registering the blankness Marisa produced as a result of the asking. Ah, he thought, so almost nothing. "You seem to have taken to your role quite naturally."

"Don't really have much of a choice," Marisa said, and took a careful step closer, though he noticed she kept the majority of the kitchen island between them. "Aren't you a vampire?"

Jack's laptop was little help. He must have known to do more than clear his technological cache, which was another small irritation. Aguillard had hoped to glean considerably more by virtue of his visit, though Jack wasn't the only person in the house he could ask.

"What do you know of vampires?" he asked, glancing up at Marisa, who shrugged.

"Blood-sucking," she said. "Mind-reading."

"Have to be careful with mind-reading," he advised, straightening his jacket and removing a small piece of lint. "Multiple creatures are capable of it. Some fae, the occasional Japanese monster, demons..." He trailed off, observing the flicker of alarm at the word *demon*. "Ah yes, you had a visit from Ilias, didn't you? Courtesy of the Casket Girl, if I'm not mistaken."

Marisa opened her mouth, then closed it. "I guess."

"You guess?" Aguillard cocked a brow, manufacturing surprise. "Don't tell me you're not sure. Typically, the visited party is quite clear on the concept."

"I just meant—" She broke off, closing up again. "I don't actually know who sent him," she said, which meant Elisabeth had gotten to her already. "Or if anything he said was even true." That, on the other hand, was evidence of Jack.

"Demons typically do not lie, but I suppose that is understandable." Aguillard observed her another long moment, adding, "You must be struggling to find your place in all this."

Marisa glanced over her shoulder, then back at Aguillard.

"I think Jack will be up soon," she lied, seeming to have recalled her previous falsity. "He's just, you know. Around here somewhere. But you might want to come back later," she offered, forcing a smile. Her lies were restless, unlike Jack and Elisabeth, who both lied so serenely. Pacifyingly, as if said lies were meant to put all relevant parties at ease by virtue of their existence.

"You seem troubled," Aguillard noted, tilting his head. "I presume the demon threatened you in some way?"

Marisa's mind called forth a far more terrifying version of Ilias, looming and threatening, along with a sense of... impending doom? Almost certainly. She seemed a woman mildly concerned with her own destruction, though not particularly aware of its nature.

"What exactly are demons?" Marisa asked, which was a surprise to Aguillard. He hadn't expected her to be forthright, but it seemed she was more indulgent with her own curiosities than he'd expected. Certainly more than Oscalia ever was. "Jack sort of gave me the impression that they're hard to kill," she clarified, "but if all it took was a stab, then—"

Aguillard chuckled. A stab, indeed. "A bit more to it than that. Demons are partway between mortal and deity," he explained. "Incorporeal, where mortals are occupants of bodies."

Marisa frowned. "But the one who came here—"

"Oh, Ilias *had* a physical form," Aguillard confirmed, "but he did not *belong* to it. You, for example, are quite different. Should anything harm your body, your thoughts will cease. Such is the manner of living for a mortal. A demon may have a body or not," he explained with a shrug, "but the harming of the body does nothing to harm that which the demon truly is."

"Which means…?"

"That killing the body is not enough," Aguillard summarized neatly. "You've heard of the law of conservation of energy?" At Marisa's nod, he continued, "A demon's energy cannot be created nor destroyed. He who kills a demon absorbs some of the demon itself, binding him to whatever remains."

Marisa seemed warily unconvinced. "What could possibly remain of a dead demon?"

"Oh, any number of things. Any remaining causes, desires, kin. Unfinished business is not only for ghosts," Aguillard advised. "It can bind any creature to this world, even after its shell has been destroyed."

"But if Jack killed Ilias—"

"Doubtful Ilias' business was unfinished. He was old, and a solitary type," Aguillard assured her. "Nor was he particularly malevolent."

"I disagree," Marisa muttered, and Aguillard caught a hint of something in her mind: an ultimatum delivered by the demon, which he plucked from her head and observed, turning it over with satisfaction.

It was one of the things Aguillard had come for, though not the only thing.

"Well," he said, resting a hand on the kitchen counter, "seeing as Jack isn't available now, I suppose I'll just have to take a room."

A little suspicion flagged at Marisa's temple, prompting her brow to furrow.

"Don't you have your own house?" Marisa asked. "Being an entrepreneur and all that."

Aguillard smiled. Good of her to recall trivialities. She would need that sort of attention to detail as things progressed.

"I do," he admitted, "but I prefer a room."

"But—"

"Didn't Jack tell you?" he cut in, leaning into the constant nudge of fragility in her head; mortals were always so sensitive when their little lives were threatened. "You can't refuse a creature."

He knew she would hear Ilias' words echo through her mind: *Death by your own hand, or by the creatures you will have wronged before the new moon is up.* Surely it kept her awake at night, which was a delicious thought. Positively ripe with possibility.

"Fine," Marisa said tightly. Displeased, it seemed, though she obligingly led him to the courtyard door. "Have a room, then."

By the time Jack got home, it was late in the afternoon. It had been a difficult morning; the problem of narrowing Elisabeth Clavier's sphere of influence was hard enough—her crimes were considered kindnesses to some, which meant she had some degree of community protection—and redrawing the magical boundaries in the city was positively draining. It was harder to control now, much less responsive, and people never cared for the disturbance of the shifts as he worked. At least three familiars had watched Jack cast in silence, tails flicking in patently feigned disinterest as if he wouldn't know perfectly well what it looked like when normal cats were lurking.

Witches in this city were relentlessly nosy. Probably with good reason, but still.

He returned to the Caretaker's house to find Marisa waiting for him in the kitchen, testy with something.

Impatience, it seemed. "Something bothering you?" he asked her, brushing her hair back from her shoulder as he approached, and she looked up at him with irritation.

"That friend of yours came here," she said. "He gives me the creeps."

'Friend' was a word rarely applied to anyone Jack knew. "Friend?"

"The bar owner. Aguillard."

"What?" The slip of audible surprise escaped him without much forethought. "Why?"

"I don't know," Marisa said listlessly, "but I don't like it."

Jack didn't like it, either. Not that he wanted her to know that. "You let him in?" he asked, hoping for something that sounded close to normal, but his pretense was mostly lost on her. She was agitated enough already without him peppering the situation with his own concerns.

"What choice did I have? You told me yourself I can't refuse him," she grumpily pointed out, "so what was I supposed to do?"

Aguillard would have known that, unfortunately. "Where did he go? In the house, I mean."

"He was in the kitchen, mostly," Marisa said, gesturing ambiguously. "He opened your laptop."

That was fine. Jack knew better than to leave active enchantments lying around. "Where else?"

"He asked for a room." That, on the other hand, was highly questionable. "I gave him one, so I assume he's in there now."

Jack's mouth went a little dry. "He's still here? How long?" he asked, and Marisa glanced over her shoulder, eyeing the clock.

"Maybe twenty minutes? Not sure. Where were you, by the way?" she asked tangentially, though Jack was too busy panicking to listen.

It wasn't like Aguillard needed a room—or, for that matter, a Caretaker. What exactly was he here to find? He obviously hadn't found it yet, if he had decided to stay, so that was a good thing.

A less-good thing, however?

That something was obviously strange about the house's enchantments if someone like Aguillard could so easily waltz in.

Jack realized with a start that Marisa was still looking at him expectantly. "What?"

"Where were you?" she said, with an air of repetition. "I had more than one unpleasant visitor while you were gone."

I have more to worry about than the quality of your visitors was on the tip of Jack's tongue, but thankfully, it didn't escape him. "I was taking care of Elisabeth. For your sake," he added pointedly, and Marisa's expression soured.

"Is that so?"

He couldn't imagine why she sounded so accusing. "Yes, it's so. Of course."

"And what makes you so sure Elisabeth is a threat to me?"

It took a moment to register that Marisa's mood was about more than just Aguillard's presence. "Hang on," Jack said, frowning. "Are you angry with me?"

She gave him a look he had formerly associated with Elisabeth. "Seriously, Jack? Some demon shows up to tell me I'm going to die less than twenty-four hours ago," Marisa growled, "and you're asking if I'm angry that you left me here alone?"

Naturally, she would fail to understand that she was hardly the center of all this.

"I'm trying to help you, Marisa," Jack said, hearing his own agitation start to creep in as he answered. "To do that, I can't just be trapped in here all the time—"

"Is there something you're not telling me?" Marisa cut in, impatient. "About this, the house, about

133

everything. People are coming after me," she reminded him, and before he could answer, she had amended with a humorless laugh, "No, no. Not people—*creatures*. They seem to want something to do with *me*, specifically," she muttered, emphatic in her bitterness, "but are you ever going to tell me what that is? Even your friend Aguillard seemed to know something I didn't—"

"What did Aguillard say?" Jack asked warily, though he doubted that would help. Aguillard would have read into more than just Marisa's answer, and unhelpfully, there was really no way to tell her he wasn't exactly Jack's friend without revealing a little too much in the process.

"Are you even listening to me?"

It was difficult to believe she'd been in bed with him (and quite affectionately, too) only the previous night. It normally took longer for women to start resenting him, but by the look on Marisa's face, Jack supposed the Caretaker was always going to be a special case.

Unfortunately, neither of them had the time for this. He needed to understand the situation more fully before it escalated beyond his control.

"Just let me talk to Aguillard," Jack said, offering a conciliatory kiss to her forehead. "Just trust me, okay? I'll tell you everything, eventually. I just have to make sure he's not—" He broke off, hesitant to worry her prematurely. "I just have to talk to him," he amended, hoping opacity would help, though it never did.

It certainly didn't this time. Marisa didn't pull away, but she didn't look any more relieved, either. "Go, then," she said, evasive. "The third room, second floor."

The rules of normal mortal relationships, even the new ones, dictated that Jack stay to say things (what's wrong?, are you okay?, don't be angry sweetheart, etc. etc.), but surely Marisa would come to learn that the two of them could never be conventional. Short of saying so aloud, Jack nodded and slipped into the courtyard, making his way to the guest house as Marisa closed the door, disappearing from sight.

"Lise," Genevieve said, and Elisabeth looked up. "Someone for you."

By the look on Genevieve's face, it wasn't someone dangerous. "I'm busy, Gen," she said, flipping the pages in the leather diary she'd been scouring all afternoon.

Then, after a moment, there was a small, meticulous throat cough.

"Too busy for me?"

Elisabeth looked up to find that Genevieve had left Marisa Marrero waiting in the door frame, leaning against the wood. Elisabeth, genuinely taken by surprise, struggled to hide her reaction. Not her favorite thing, surprises.

"Yes," she said, though she conceded to wait a moment, biding her time before saying more. "How'd you find me?"

Marisa tossed a book down on the bed in Elisabeth's temporary quarters.

"Ah," Elisabeth said. "Fair enough."

It was the same book on New Orleans' history that Marisa had been perusing that first night, when they'd run into each other in the speakeasy. Someone had done their reading about vampires in the city, it seemed.

"You're the Casket Girl, aren't you?" Marisa asked rhetorically. She obviously already knew that; Elisabeth observed that Marisa had also slid the door shut behind her, making this at least partly clandestine. "I figured I couldn't go wrong with the Ursuline Convent."

"I do have an apartment," Elisabeth said. "Unfortunately, I can't go there now, seeing as your boyfriend blacklisted me."

Marisa's mouth twitched at the mention of Jack. "Blacklisted?"

"Means I'm fair game," Elisabeth supplied with a shrug. "No consequences if someone kills me or my sisters." She permitted herself to smile thinly. "I welcome them to try, of course, but still. No need to make things unnecessarily straightforward."

"Oh." Marisa shrank a little, losing some of her nerve. "I'm sorry."

Elisabeth shook her head. "Don't apologize for Jack. It wouldn't be enough coming from you, first of all, and secondly, I didn't ask for an apology. His method of survival just…" Another shrug. "Is what it is."

Marisa hesitated. "But given your history—"

"Yes, we have a long one. Of which love was a relatively small piece." To Elisabeth's amusement, Marisa flinched. "Upset to hear he loved me?" she guessed.

Marisa said nothing.

"Understandable," Elisabeth mused. Was she taunting Marisa for a reason? Unclear, even to herself. "I suppose it's easier on your conscience if you believe he never really did," she continued, "but that's not how it works. Love simply lives and dies, like anything else."

"No. No, it's not that, I just—" Marisa stopped again, taking a few paces around Elisabeth's room to let the conversation settle to the floor. "I thought the convent was supposed to have some sort of anti-vampire measures," she observed, not-so-subtly changing the subject. "Isn't that what the nails were blessed for?"

A common misconception. "Funny thing about that. Keeps a lot of things away, but not so much creatures. Not awesome for my skin," Elisabeth admitted, "but it makes this place sort of an impenetrable fortress to most types of magic. Certainly any supernatural kinds."

Marisa frowned. "So, you're... mortal here?"

"Close enough to it," Elisabeth said. "Powerless, anyway. But the upside is knowing that anyone who comes in here is no better off than I am. And before you say anything," she added with a darkened laugh, "Jack already knows that. It's not a secret, so telling him wouldn't help."

Marisa looked alarmed by the suggestion. "I'm not here to spy on you. Actually, I'm," she began hastily, and then hesitated. "I have a problem, I think."

Elisabeth rose to her feet, relocating from the little desk at the edge of the room to perch on the side of her bed. "You have a number of problems, Caretaker," she observed. "You just slept with Jack St. Germaine, in case you forgot, which is probably chief among them."

Marisa's cheeks burned furiously. "It's not that. It's—" A pause. "Do you know Aguillard?"

"Who, the bar owner? Yes," Elisabeth said, scowling to think of him. "He works for Jack. Does his bidding, as far as I can tell." She picked at a loose thread on the duvet, adding, "He's the political arm of Jack's influence. Jack's the rotator cuff."

It was fairly obvious that Marisa was struggling with whatever she wanted to say, or to not say. She stood in silence for a moment, contemplating her shoes, and Elisabeth sighed impatiently.

"You do realize I don't have all day, don't you?" she prompted, and Marisa's gaze snapped up. "And even if I did, *you* certainly don't. The moment a creature needs you, you'll have to go, so if you needed to ask me something—"

"What does it mean?" Marisa blurted, sounding more than a little pained by the asking. "This... Caretaker thing, what does it mean? I... *feel* things," she stammered, "and I seem to be drawing these creatures to me, but I... I can't explain it, and—"

She faltered, helpless, and Elisabeth sighed.

"You have the potential to become very powerful," Elisabeth confirmed, and Marisa nodded, tentatively grateful. She seemed relieved to be getting an answer, however unhelpful it might be. "I assume that's what you're feeling?" Elisabeth guessed. "Magic?" At Marisa's hesitation, Elisabeth explained, "Power is never gained or lost. It can, however, accumulate. Remnants of it, anyway."

Marisa sank onto the opposite edge of Elisabeth's bed, contemplating that. "And what does that have to do with me?"

"You're a receptacle for what comes and goes," Elisabeth said. "Creatures are messy, really. Most of them possess power by accident, or by some chance mutation, so faint traces of it fall away. You know, like dead skin. Hair. Dandruff." She shrugged again. "It's really a little disgusting if you think about it, so try not to—but still, it's not like it can just settle into nothing. It's grime that needs somewhere to go."

Marisa made a face, obviously thinking about precisely the thing Elisabeth had warned her not to. "So, what I'm feeling, it's... magic remnants?"

"Something like that, yes."

"And I'm tied to the house because of... my blood?"

"Your bloodline," Elisabeth corrected, "most likely. I don't know, exactly, but I would guess your acceptance of the house is part of it. You must have consented to your role," she added, "or you wouldn't be accumulating its power."

"But," Marisa began, and swallowed. "But what if I don't want it? Power, I mean."

Elisabeth glanced at the leather book on her desk, then back at Marisa.

"I don't know," she said, and when Marisa opened her mouth to protest, Elisabeth shook her head. "I really don't; I'm not just saying that. I know a lot of things, but not that. Jack would know," she admitted, and Marisa's expression darkened. "He's the one who understands magic, how to cultivate it, how to use it. I'm just undead."

"You know a lot for 'just' undead," Marisa remarked, and Elisabeth rolled her eyes.

"I read," she said. "And besides, you don't just exist for over two centuries without some effort to understand what the fuck you even are."

Marisa seemed unconvinced. "Why do you know so much about me, then?"

"Because you're not a secret. The Caretaker's house is the supernatural meridian in the city," Elisabeth explained. "You're the line between sides. One side belongs to Jack and Aguillard, and the other—" She broke off, still less than thrilled to admit it. "The other used to belong to us. But it figures," she remarked with a bitter laugh. "We were here first, and per usual, they've burned us out."

Marisa, relieved to finally have answers, couldn't seem to stop asking questions, even in the face of Elisabeth's obvious reluctance to answer.

"You told me not to trust Jack," Marisa pressed, shifting closer to Elisabeth. "Does that mean I shouldn't trust Aguillard, either?"

"I wouldn't. But I don't think it matters," Elisabeth said. She observed with subtle interest the way Marisa had leaned towards her in her plea. Desperation clearly had pitched Marisa forward, but whether she wanted information or something else entirely, Elisabeth didn't know.

Nor did she plan to find out, either. Unlike Aguillard, Elisabeth wasn't in the business of invading a mortal's mind; if Marisa wanted her to know something, she'd have to say it aloud, and who knew if the Caretaker had the stones for that.

"You already have Jack," Elisabeth pointed out, "so as long as you don't cross him, I wouldn't worry about Aguillard."

"What if I do cross him? Jack, I mean."

Elisabeth sighed. *He'll try to kill you, sweetie,* was probably not an answer Marisa would handle well.

"You'll suffer the consequences of that, I suppose."

"But then why did Jack bother protecting me in the first place?"

"Because he needs you." Ridiculous, really, that Marisa would even need to ask. It showed just how little she knew about herself, or about anything, really. "The more power you accumulate, Marisa, the more valuable you are. Like a talisman."

Marisa had shifted forward again, helpless. "So why not just tell me that?"

"Would you, if you were him?" Elisabeth most certainly wouldn't, if she had Jack's fondness for control; which wasn't to say she didn't, but she played her games much more beneficially.

She knew, for example, how to kill two birds with one stone.

"Powerful objects become less useful when they decide to control themselves," she cautioned Marisa, daring her to take the bait, and in response, Marisa's lips parted, then shut.

She was close, by then. Close enough that Elisabeth could see her pulse quickening, her mind turning, her breath faltering. Close enough to touch, if Elisabeth wanted to.

If she allowed it.

"How do I know you're not just saying that so you can use me?" Marisa asked softly, which was a very clever paranoia to have. Marisa, Elisabeth thought, was very clever, aside from the way she'd come in here so vulnerable.

That, and the way she'd come so unwisely close.

"Guess you'll just have to trust me," Elisabeth murmured, brushing her fingers along the inside of Marisa's arm.

A knock at the door indicated Jack had found him, so Aguillard waved a hand, permitting the latch to turn. Jack burst inside, shutting the door firmly in his wake.

"What are you doing here?" Jack hissed, scouring the room. No doubt he was feeling for tangles of magic, which of course he wouldn't find; unlike Jack, Aguillard didn't leave traces. Moreover, that wasn't what this visit had been about. "I told you, I already have the Caretaker on our side, and I'm taking care of Elisabeth—"

"Mm, yes, about that," Aguillard said, glancing over his shoulder at Jack. "Was it really necessary to *attack* her, Jack?" he sighed, facetiously lamenting. "You know she won't take kindly to that."

"I——" Jack frowned. "I didn't attack her, I'm not stupid." A more accurate point, had Aguillard cared to make it, was that Jack *couldn't* have attacked her; not very successfully, and certainly not anymore, though it was understandable if he was unwilling to say so aloud. As far as the rest of the creatures knew, Jack's supremacy remained unchallenged.

Which was precisely why their partnership was such a convenient little lie until it wasn't.

(For Jack, anyway.)

"I was working on the city's perimeters," Jack said, waving somewhere over his shoulder in reference. "Making sure she and her sisters don't try to cross any lines."

Jack's mind, like always, was preoccupied with Elisabeth's face. Funny, Aguillard thought, that Jack could only see Elisabeth Clavier two ways: one as she was in his bed—pliable and soft, warm and tender—and the other cold, teeth bared, blood beneath her black-painted nails to match the crimson traces on her lips. What a dichotomy it was, loving her and hating her. A lifelong wish to either possess or destroy a woman with no in-between was, as far as Aguillard could see from Jack's experience, tiresome indeed.

"Well, *someone* did something," Aguillard said, tutting softly in disapproval. "Why else would she have gone to Ursuline?"

Jack blinked at the mention of the Ursuline Convent—which was an unconventional fortress, but a fortress, nonetheless. It was where the Casket Girls typically regrouped, plotting their little acts of terror. Elisabeth Clavier was militarizing for something, most likely, and for Jack, the usual tiny flicker of fear had manifested behind his temples, mixing in with guilt.

(It was always both fear and remorse when it came to Elisabeth; Jack was incapable of feeling only one or the other when it came to his former paramour.)

"Aguillard," Jack said hoarsely. "Please tell me you didn't."

Aguillard returned his attention where it had been. The conversation had already grown wearying, more so than he'd predicted, and it wasn't as if he had any answers Jack would care to hear. It certainly wasn't why he had come here.

In the absence of an answer, Aguillard heard Jack groan in frustration.

"Don't touch Marisa," he warned, yanking open the door.

"Don't be ridiculous, Jack," Aguillard returned impassively. "I have no interest in your latest liaison."

The door shut without a response, Jack's footsteps fading as he returned to the courtyard.

"Now," Aguillard said, "where were we?"

In response, Oscalia Marrero, former Caretaker and current ghost, flickered unhappily in place. She was dressed in the same clothes she'd been wearing upon her death; not for the first time, Aguillard wondered if she might eventually come to thank him for not spoiling her afterlife with bloodstains.

"I believe you were agreeing to say nothing," Aguillard prompted. "Correct?"

"I can see you now," Oscalia replied. She was a moody sort of ghost, always melancholy. "For so many years, I thought you existed only in my head."

"Well, that's your fault," Aguillard reminded her. "You were the one who refused the power provided to you, you know. You might not have lost your sight if you hadn't resisted it so pointlessly."

"I had a husband, Aguillard. A son." Melancholy, melodrama. The afterlife was so unrepentantly dreary. "You took them from me."

"Incorrect. You sent them away," Aguillard reminded her, already resentful of the conversation. How many times would it have to be had? Apparently, the occasions it had taken place over Oscalia's lifetime were not sufficient to make it clear. "You saw the power as an infection, and you tried, pointlessly, to cure it. Foolish of you." Aguillard slid a hand over the furniture, observing the dust that collected at his fingertips. "Your granddaughter, I suspect, will not be so stupid to resist."

"I did my job. No more, no less."

Laughable, really. "On the contrary, if you'd done your job, Oscalia, you'd still be alive."

"You asked too much of me." The ghost flickered with sorrow.

Tiresome.

"First I ask too much, now I ask too little," Aguillard said impatiently. "Your occupation here is not my concern. I need nothing further from you."

"You require my silence," Oscalia reminded him.

Aguillard waved a hand. "That presumes you figure out how to make anyone realize you're here to begin with—which is, at best, a longshot."

"You cannot harm these creatures, Aguillard, or they will come for my granddaughter. For Marisa."

Ah, so he was getting through to her, then. Finally. "Yes, they will, won't they?" he reminded her spiritedly. "So, you see the purpose behind all this, then? The more souls tied to this house, the more power it has. The more use it is to me. And I," he concluded, "unlike my sister Delphine, will not waste my time soiling worthless mortals to do it."

Delphine LaLaurie, Madame Blanque or whatever silly human thing she had called herself, had been an idiot, of course. Sadism for entertainment was messy and useless, particularly the way she'd gone about it. Serial killing, fine, but to what end? What good was a mortal when it was gone?

Certainly nothing compared to what remained after the death of a *creature*.

Before him, Oscalia's image waned. "Marisa is a mortal," she whispered, as if Aguillard might have forgotten the obvious.

"Not for much longer. She's a pail waiting to be filled. And between Elisabeth Clavier and Jack St. Germaine, she's bound to give in soon enough."

"She's clever," Oscalia said. "I watch her. She's no fool."

Ah, the blessed optimism of death; if only it weren't so charmingly annoying. Aguillard had business to attend to and a bar to open very shortly, so Oscalia certainly wasn't helping to keep him on schedule. If she couldn't be convinced, then she would have to simply... go away, at least temporarily.

"You know, if you really wanted your granddaughter to stand a chance in this city, you would have taught her how to recognize a demon when she saw one," Aguillard said, and the moment he directed his incorporeal will in the direction of his aggrandizing host, Oscalia gave a shudder of pain, flickering from sight to disappear once again into her void of temporary oblivion.

Elisabeth's touch against Marisa's skin was soft, foreign, familiar. Marisa could still taste her kiss from that morning; already, she felt herself giving into something she belatedly hoped she hadn't wanted until that moment. She certainly hadn't *thought* it was what she wanted, not really, but then Elisabeth was leaning closer and closer, and her touch was enough to drive Marisa half insane.

"What did you really come here for?" Elisabeth said, with her usual tone of amusement. "I'm sure you could have gotten answers from Jack, had you played him correctly. Which you're apparently capable of doing."

A flash of Jack's mouth on her skin sent a shiver up Marisa's spine, magnified by Elisabeth's proximity. Was it possible to want them both? She seemed incapable of wanting one without the other—only it was just Elisabeth with her now, and that seemed to be more than enough.

Marisa forced a swallow. "Maybe I was curious."

"About?"

She envied Elisabeth's ability to conceal her expressions.

"Everything. Me. Jack." A pause. "You," she admitted, and then Elisabeth's slender fingers crept up to Marisa's tank top, running along the hem of her shoulder strap.

"Vampirically, you mean?" Elisabeth asked, sliding her tongue along the sharp edges of her teeth. She gave the strap of Marisa's shirt a nudge, letting it drape from Marisa's shoulder to her arm. "Or is it some other curiosity you have?"

Elisabeth was dressed more simply than usual. A black dress, no shoes; no elegantly constricted chignon or twist. Left down, her hair was longer than Marisa had expected, and far more faceted in the light. Without makeup, she was less garish, too; though, even without the dark red lipstick, Elisabeth looked no less intimidating than she always did.

She smelled like rose petals; dried ones. A faint perfume of sleeplessness and sweet decay.

"I don't know what I want," Marisa confessed, but she still reached for Elisabeth, who leaned forward to answer a question that hadn't been asked. Her hair fell in a curtain along Marisa's arm as her lips touched Marisa's shoulder lightly, gingerly; more an intake of breath than anything. It was all surprisingly soft, Marisa thought, even gentle, possibly tender—but then, before she knew it was happening, Elisabeth's hand was prying her legs apart, the tips of her fingers darting under the material of Marisa's denim shorts with such sudden certainty that Marisa gasped; terrified, and bizarrely, undeniably, elated.

"You have to say it," Elisabeth said, and was *she* breathless, too? Or was it really only Marisa who couldn't breathe? Elisabeth's fingers had paused against the material of her underwear and it was everything Marisa could do not to move; not to answer with a shift of her hips. Not to hold Elisabeth's palm flat against her and beg her for friction, expressing some uncharted desire she didn't fully understand.

"You have to tell me where you want me to touch you, if you want me to," Elisabeth said to the side of Marisa's neck, and the tiniest motion of her fingers drew Marisa's underwear aside. Her touch floated there, airy and impossibly delicate, while her lips brushed Marisa's jaw. "You'll have to ask me, Marisa. I keep telling you," Elisabeth said, teeth grazing over the lobe of Marisa's ear, "you have to take what you want."

Elisabeth's skin against hers was like a chill, a shudder. This sort of intimacy was murder waiting to happen; one motion, little more than an inch, and Elisabeth's teeth could sink into her throat. One wrong move and the light could go out, and all desire for anything could easily cease.

Gently, in answer to her thoughts, Elisabeth's tongue slipped across Marisa's carotid artery. A little lick, and then a scrape of canines. Marisa felt her breath grow ragged, and Elisabeth's hand shifted again, forcing Marisa to a voiceless, helpless mewl of, "Please."

Elisabeth's lips twisted against Marisa's skin. "Please what?"

"Please touch me," Marisa forced out, and to her dismay, Elisabeth drew her hand away, abruptly releasing her. She leaned back, dark eyes on Marisa's face, and slipped the tip of her pink tongue between her lips, retreating to recline against the pillows.

The hem of Elisabeth's black dress had ridden up on her thigh, nearly to her hip.

"Touch me yourself," she said.

Before Marisa could recall her ability to refuse, she had already crawled to Elisabeth on the bed, finding her mouth with a gasp.

Aguillard inspected his fingernails, flicking a bit of dried blood away. He straightened from the body of the shape-shifting creature who had arrived in the shape of a young girl, watching it morph slowly back to its usual foxlike form as power slowly seeped into the walls.

From the corner of his eye, he caught a flicker of something.

"You're back," he noted to Oscalia, glancing sideways. "Learned your lesson?"

She said nothing, and he glanced at his watch.

"Probably enough for now," he assured her. "Evening rush will start soon."

Aguillard was primarily a businessman, and there was inventory to be accounted for. Customers, clients; people who were looking for leadership in these dark times. Elisabeth Clavier was in hiding, after all. Jack St. Germaine had killed a demon.

Things weren't safe in New Orleans, and it was Aguillard's job to reassure them.

"How many did you kill this time?" Oscalia asked him dully, and Aguillard adjusted his collar, removing a bit of lint.

"Enough for the time being," he said, and removed a handkerchief from his pocket.

Better he didn't dirty his hands with whatever grime had been left on the door.

"Get out," Genevieve said coldly, which was, quite unfortunately, about what Jack had expected.

"It wasn't me," he repeated for at least the third time, frustrated by her obvious apathy. Of all the Casket Girls who might have come to the door, Genevieve was by far the worst and least helpful option. "You have to let me in, Gen. I have to tell her it wasn't me—"

"Great," Genevieve replied, turning away. "I'll be sure to pass the message along."

"It had to have been Aguillard!" Jack shouted after her, frustrated and helpless. He couldn't do anything useful from outside the walls of the Ursuline Convent; he couldn't even persuade Genevieve to see reason. "Don't you get it?" he asked, half-pleading. "He must be playing us against each other—first with Ilias, then this… *attack*, whatever he did—don't you see it?"

Genevieve spun, lips pressed thin. "Who ordered the blacklist?" she demanded, as Jack grimaced. "We all know it was you, Jack. What does it matter whether you were the one who attacked Lise or not? You still gave the world permission to do it."

"But he's clearly playing the fringe creatures against the establishment," Jack insisted, and Genevieve rolled her eyes, turning away again. "Gen, listen to me, he's not what you think he is! You have to trust me; you have to tell Elisabeth," he called after her, gratified to see her pause. "She'll know I'm telling the truth!"

Judging by the rigid line of Genevieve's spine, that had been precisely the wrong thing to say.

"I think Elisabeth has trusted you for long enough," Genevieve said coldly.

Then she continued away, leaving Jack to kick angrily at the ground, swearing.

Fucking Aguillard. Bad enough that Jack had been keeping secrets as it was; now Aguillard was intentionally acting *against* Jack, which meant Jack was losing his usefulness. Either that, or Aguillard suspected he no longer needed Jack, which certainly wasn't good.

Elisabeth could have done something about it. That must have been why Aguillard played them against each other.

He had to speak to her, and soon.

Jack hurried back to the Caretaker's house. Whatever Aguillard was up to, he hoped it hadn't somehow come down on Marisa.

The floral scent of Elisabeth's hair lingered on the pillowcase, filling Marisa's nose as she rested her cheek against the fabric. With her eyes closed, she could feel nothing but Elisabeth's weight on her spine; the curves of Elisabeth's skin were like velvet where they were tangled up, bare limbs and twisted sheets, amid the still and somber air.

Something hitched in Marisa's chest, disrupting her tranquility. Her feet twitched, static rising in her ears. Beneath the bed, the earth rumbled, though she seemed to be the only one who felt it. Something was growing restless; she was needed somewhere else.

Apparently the convent didn't prevent all types of magic.

"You said," Marisa began, and stopped, eyes fluttering open as she considered how to say it. "You said lives were meant to be taken back," she murmured to Elisabeth, clearing a little stirring of disquietude from her throat.

In answer, the bone of Elisabeth's ankle traced the outside of Marisa's calf.

Go on, I'm listening.

"Will it be like this forever?" Marisa whispered.

It was slow and contemplative between them now. Not the feverish arrhythmia it had been, cold hands on hot skin and warm breaths trapped in wild hair.

"There's only one thing you can do," Elisabeth said eventually, resting her chin at the top of Marisa's spine. "This thing, the Caretaker, the house... it's not natural, which means there's only one person in the city powerful enough to have done it." She brushed her lips against Marisa's shoulder, fingers covetously tracing her waist. "If you want to free yourself from the contract you accepted, Marisa, then you have to destroy the enchantment's source. The person who cast it."

Marisa tensed a little, angling her head to look at Elisabeth.

"Are you telling me I have to kill Jack?"

If that had been Elisabeth's plan all along, she didn't bother to hide it.

"Yes," she said, dark eyes glinting as the sun faded solemnly outside the convent windows.

PART V: The Ghost

For the woman who was once Oscalia Marrero, death had been like waking from a dream.

That the former Caretaker had ever had a life, a husband and a son, seemed so distant as to be imaginary; more a glimmer of a daydream than a past. Long before Oscalia had grown unable to control the power surges that expelled from her body in seizures, moments of acute paralysis, and temporary (that eventually became permanent) blindness, the sweat of possessing so much accumulating magic had already caused her to live in a state of near-constant fever. By the time she had been

unable to suppress a live tremor in her hands, nearly
dropping her infant son to the floor, she had come to
understand there could be no escaping it. There could be
no mind over matter, not here, and if the physical
limitations were not bad enough, her visions of the future
only plagued her further, taunting her with some
indefinable pain that promised it was yet to come.

She resented the power, which had not only robbed
her of her life and her marriage but also stolen from her
own body like a virus, like a cancer. It seemed to
replicate in her cells, like an illness. She had tried once or
twice to take it, to control it, but the rare moments of
using it had been like permitting a gun to fire without
direction; as difficult to aim as live ammunition, and
impossible to retract once it had been unleashed. Worse,
to use it felt like the most unpleasant of bodily functions.
She was drained, ill and unable to eat or drink, for days
after attempting it. It was a magic that was not only
happy to occupy her as a host, but also to drain her,
parasitically. It did not want to be used, refined, or
channeled. It wanted only to use *her*, as if she were
nothing but a limb.

It had been Oscalia's father who'd left her the house.
Hardly the first man to abandon his wife and child
without further contact, Cornelio had been a mystery to

both Oscalia and her mother until his death, when his executor arrived with oddly specific instructions: that Cornelio's daughter and only living heir was to enter the bequeathed house by stepping onto the threshold, with both feet, on the eve of a new moon.

Oscalia remembered walking inside the house, which had been unassuming—even derelict—from the outside, revealing a surprising grandness within. She remembered making her way across the floor, the lights flickering without switches; the enormous crystal chandelier, the Victorian portrait, the elegant porcelain bust. Her fiancé had been reluctant to sell the house like they had originally planned, finding it charming and altogether more than they could ever afford to buy on his working-class salary alone. Instead, he insisted they move into it themselves, exclaiming that it would be a marvelous home to start a family. Oscalia, already sensing something ominous about the house that she couldn't explain, had loved her sweetheart too much to refute his enthusiasm. She allowed herself to be carried off on his excitement, assuming the guest house would provide a stable enough income if she made it available for tourists and vacationers, as her father had presumably done.

Jack had come along shortly after, introducing himself as a friend of her father's, though he hardly looked old enough to be. A perpetually handsome man even after Oscalia had grown stooped and haggard, Jack St. Germaine became a frequent visitor to the house, ingratiating himself with Oscalia's husband and soothing what she thought, at first, were her pregnancy hormones, or possibly some pre-maternal anxiety. It wasn't until she revealed her state to Jack that he told her the truth, both about what her father's role had been and about the details of what he'd left out. Aside from failing to inform her of the nature of her supernatural guests, Cornelio, a lifelong bachelor, had failed to inform Oscalia of a crucial caveat in the house's enchantments: that while *she* was protected from any ill will or malevolence, her husband and future child were not. The privilege of safety belonged solely to the Caretaker.

The fighting began over secrecy. Oscalia would tell her husband Lucian the truth about the occupants of the guest house and watch him forget it. The holes in his memory were filled, instead, with imaginary recollections of various betrayals, including nonexistent infidelities with Jack. Oscalia's reassurances, her protests and tearful promises that she had done no such thing, drained from her husband's mind each morning as if she'd never told him anything at all. His displeasure festered; the little bits of magic in the house snuck into his ears and infected his mind the same way it did with Oscalia's, but closer to poison. The magic, or whatever it was, clearly did not want Lucian in the house, or her son, either, whom she had named for his father. Baby Luc would scream from the night terrors Oscalia knew were more real than Lucian believed, though he only blamed her for being an inadequate mother.

They couldn't stay, and she couldn't leave without being called back. When Lucian finally stormed out with the baby in tow, she considered it a painful relief.

She went blind long before Aguillard found her. He had followed some invisible trail to land at her door, observing the twists and tangles that leached from her vitals. By that time, she considered the house's power to be another entity, existing in tandem beside her. That it would have formed its own body after sapping her of her strength seemed inevitable, and it was only when Oscalia overheard an argument that she realized Aguillard was not the same magic she had lived beside for decades, but rather, something else.

"You killed my sister, did you not? Surely you understood that killing a demon does not end there. Or did you wonder how you became like this, suddenly filled with more raw power than you could ever use? Did the sensation of your magic expanding not concern you?"

It was Jack's arrogant voice that replied, "You cannot possibly think to threaten me further. With everything I've already done?"

"I'm aware of what you've done, and I seem to understand it better than you do, as well. You only made a mess of things before me; getting yourself banished by the Casket Girl, forced to disappear from prominence, even after establishing such an extravagant reputation. You haven't had the same control for decades; not since before that girl leaping from your window, hm?"

At Jack's silence, the voice that was Aguillard's continued, "Admit it, Jack. Your powers have long exceeded your control, and given the error you made with this house——"

"The house does not concern you, Aguillard."

"Oh," Aguillard scoffed, "so you *meant* to chain your alchemical abilities to the bloodline of your house and its Caretaker, then? That certainly wasn't my sister's power getting the better of you, I'm sure——"

"What exactly do you want?"

There was an air of resignation to Jack's voice, which Oscalia had never heard before, and was quite disconcerted to hear now.

"Well, I want you to admit the truth, *Jacques*. That you've been playing the role of alchemist for centuries, only to find that you scarcely know what real power there is in the world. That you're under the thumb of a blood-sucking misandrist who is, aside from all this leaking magic, your greatest weakness and your most dangerous rival all at once. I want you to admit that this house *and* its keeper are impelled by your very existence," Aguillard said with a laugh, "and then I want you to admit that the magic inside it, the same magic I possess, grows more each day, festering into power too strong for even you to use it. Or did you misunderstand the meaning of demonic possession?"

Oscalia sucked in a breath, startled by understanding. So the voice and the house's magic had both belonged to a demon, then. That explained its nature, needy and greedy and infectious, latching on and sucking the life from any who occupied its walls.

"I can cut myself off from the house," Jack warned. "That's the purpose of the Caretaker—it relies on me, not the other way around."

"Not if you're not alive," Aguillard replied with a laugh. "If you're gone, the magic goes with you, and there's a difference between longevity and immortality, Jack. You're old, not invulnerable—not to mention that your power is rapidly being taken over by what remains of my sister's, and if anyone knew what I know…"

Aguillard paused. "In fact, come to think of it," he mused knowingly, "if Elisabeth Clavier knew what I know about the demon you mistakenly lured into her city, do *you* think she'd hesitate to kill you?"

Even Oscalia could see that Aguillard had made a compelling point.

"Fine," Jack said through his teeth. "What will it take to keep you quiet?"

"Free rein," said Aguillard, and though Oscalia did not know what that meant, she certainly knew it was going to be trouble.

The moment she was able, Oscalia made her way blindly to the kitchen, searching through drawers for items to carefully stow away; a knife by her bed, a hammer in the bathroom, rusted shears in the garden. Something that meant the next time she saw Jack St. Germaine, she could sever herself from him, precisely as Aguillard had said. She could kill him and be done; she had no idea how long it had been, but if there was still a husband and son to return to, or a life she could regain by freeing herself from the house's constraints, then—

"Ah, ah, ah," said the voice that belonged to Aguillard, snatching up Oscalia's hand as she tried to secure a knife below the kitchen counter. "What's this, hm?"

He floated into her head, probing around the way the house's magic so often did.

"So," Aguillard murmured, "you're going to kill Jack to free yourself? Sorry, Caretaker, I can't allow you to do that. I have him where I want him, you see? He'll work for me now, keep my hands clean," he said softly, "and no one has to know what I am, or that my sister's power grows in me. Cushy arrangement, isn't it? And I'm afraid I can't permit you to intervene."

Oscalia struggled against his grip, feeling the sensation of his hold on her warping from human to incorporeal, pressure mounting somewhere in her throat until she could no longer manage to breathe.

Then, when she opened her eyes, it was as if she had woken from a deep and terrifying slumber, a spark of what she was resuming its occupancy where the house's magic had once been.

Oscalia had evaporated from the house like it had never contained her, now both freed and trapped, but that had not been her concern. Instead, the moment that struck her with a breath of fear was the one upon realizing that Aguillard, who stood over her body, was bending to watch something seep out of her body and

into the floors, glowing faintly in knots below the cracks
of the wood. It was as if in death, some part of what
she'd come to possess—the pockets of power here and
there, like the voices that gifted her the visions—had
flowed back into the house, collecting in invisible
currents.

"Interesting," Aguillard murmured to himself.

Then he looked up, spotting Oscalia's ghost, and
smiled thinly.

"I think we'll be needing a new Caretaker," Aguillard
had informed her, summoning a paper and pen.

Marisa woke with a start, temporarily lost in time and
space as she found herself in unfamiliar quarters once
again. "Shit," she exhaled, forcing herself upright. "Did I
fall asleep?"

Elisabeth looked up from where she was curled
around herself at her desk, knees pulled into her chest as
she pored over that same leather-bound journal. "Yes,"
she said, returning her attention to the notes. She turned
a page, frowning at something, and said, "You should
probably head back soon. I imagine Jack will be
wondering where you are."

Marisa reached down for her shorts, identifying the separate locations of her shoes where they'd been discarded on the floor. "How long was I out?"

"Not long. Half an hour." Elisabeth turned another page, skimming it, then looked up, observing Marisa for a long moment. "Have you decided what you're going to do?"

Marisa stiffened, pretending not to. "About what?"

"Anything." Elisabeth set down the journal with a shrug, releasing each leg individually to stretch slowly, languidly, upwards. "Jack, for one," she exhaled, rising to her feet to join Marisa, "or, for that matter, yourself."

"I'm not killing him," Marisa said again, closing her eyes as Elisabeth's fingers danced up the vertebrae at the back of her neck. "*You* may hate him—"

"Who says I hate him?"

As if it wasn't perfectly obvious. "The point is, Elisabeth, I'm not doing it. I'll find some other way to make this work. I don't need Jack *gone*, I just…" She trailed off, feeling Elisabeth settle on the bed behind her. "I don't know what I want," Marisa admitted, as Elisabeth shifted her wild hair to one side, resting a chin on her shoulder.

"Ah," Elisabeth murmured, "so I should interpret all these spontaneous visits as… casual sex, then?"

The soft scent of her hair crept through Marisa's conscience, disrupting it.

"You say that like you want more," Marisa said.

Elisabeth chuckled. "Maybe I do."

"No, you don't." Marisa turned sharply, facing Elisabeth. "You want me to kill Jack."

Elisabeth arched a brow. "And?"

"And, that's it. That's the whole thing. You want Jack dead, end of story."

"Sweetheart, if I simply wanted Jack dead, I would not need you to do it," Elisabeth informed her, leaning back on her elbows. "I'm not in the business of hiring assassins when I could do the job perfectly well myself."

There she was again: confident, sharp as a knife, relentlessly brutal. Elisabeth Clavier, Casket Girl, head vampiress and supernatural mercenary. Much as Marisa hated to admit it, the most irresistible parts of Elisabeth were also the coldest ones. The more difficult she was to reach, the more Marisa unwisely did it, finding herself leaning towards Elisabeth until she had abandoned the effort at putting on her shoes. Elisabeth's lips, meanwhile, made soft, indecent suggestions to the hollow of Marisa's throat.

"You," Marisa began, and swallowed. "You don't want me."

"Oh, I beg to differ," Elisabeth said, tugging Marisa closer and taking a fistful of her hair, smiling darkly. "Or is there some other way you wish to be wanted?"

Guilelessly, Marisa thought. Wholly, purely.

Or at least without wondering if murder was expected in return.

"What if I had feelings for you?" Marisa asked her quietly, and Elisabeth paused the progression of her kisses, leaning away for a moment before disentangling herself and moving elsewhere on the bed. "See?" Marisa said, gesturing bitterly to the distance between them. "You can't even hear me say the words without panicking."

Elisabeth, however, seemed to consider Marisa with a new-old meanness.

"*Do* you have feelings for me?" Elisabeth said, and it felt like a rebuttal. A challenge. "Explain to me how that would work, Marisa. Should I devote myself to you, then?" she mused, nastily mocking. "Should I just go into hiding with my beautiful mortal lover, locked away inside a convent with nothing but each other until you grow old and I don't?"

She kicked away from Marisa, resting her feet on the floor. "You've been reading too many romance novels," she scoffed. "Spend a couple of months in New Orleans and suddenly you expect to have your own undead seductress to pleasure you at your whim."

Marisa bristled. "That's not what I meant; I'm just saying—"

"I know what you're saying. Though, a thought," Elisabeth posed, giving Marisa a cold look of warning. "If I went into your thoughts right now, Marisa, would I find Jack inside your head?"

I know things have been wrong between us lately, Jack reminded her, his blue eyes manifesting in Marisa's memory, *but you understand, don't you? I never expected to feel this way; I haven't felt this way for years, decades. Centuries, even.*

She saw his hands, coaxing her back; felt her face between his palms until she could taste his words on her lips. *Marisa, give me a chance to show you that this, whatever exists between us, it's not an accident.*

She blinked away the heat of Jack's mouth, the pressure of his hips. The instant rush of guilt that had sent her half-running back to Ursuline's, to say *Elisabeth, I can't do this*, until then it was *Elisabeth's* lips and *Elisabeth's* hands—Elisabeth's crimson nails on the button of Marisa's black jeans—and then it was Elisabeth's smell of roses lingering on her skin. It was the same recurring disaster of giving in, over and over, cycling between Jack and Elisabeth until shit, she was trapped from all sides.

"Thought so," Elisabeth said, observing Marisa's expression and rising to her feet. She crossed the room to pick up Marisa's other shoe, handing it to her. "Don't pretend you've earned the right to believe I'm heartless," Elisabeth suggested drily, "when you're the one who can't even make up your mind."

"But Elisabeth, I——"

She was interrupted by the little tapping in her bones; the restless sense that something was calling. The ground beneath her hummed with expectation, summoning her home. Someone—or some*thing*—was waiting for her, demanding her.

...death by your own hand, or at the hands of the creatures you will have wronged...

"Just go," Elisabeth advised neutrally, returning to her desk and the journal. "I have plenty to worry about without your personal crisis on my hands."

Marisa pulled on her shoes, chewing her lip, but struggled to think of what to say. It wasn't as if the issue was resolved.

Would it be Elisabeth or Jack?

"See you later," Elisabeth said, half-laughing, as if the inevitability of Marisa's return was a constant source of humor. Some undying joke for her undead lover.

In the end, Marisa left without saying anything, heading back to the Caretaker's house with the perfume of dead roses caught in the snares of her wild hair.

"So," Aguillard said. "You really don't think Elisabeth's gotten to your Caretaker yet?"

Jack set his jaw. "Elisabeth can do what she wants, Aguillard. I already know that whatever you're up to with Marisa, it has nothing to do with Elisabeth or me."

"And what would I be up to?" Aguillard posed genially. "I can't imagine what you might have in mind."

Jack struggled not to scowl; the fact that Jack truly *didn't* know what Aguillard was planning to do was, admittedly, driving him a bit mad. His only avenue was to press the issue; to hope the demon masquerading as a vampire might inadvertently reveal something, anything, that would give Jack a necessary leg up.

"I still keep your secrets," Jack reminded Aguillard. Another gamble, a conversational probe, though the use of emotional leverage wasn't particularly useful when applied to a creature without emotion. "If the others knew what you were—no," Jack amended with a scoff, "if they knew *who* you were, and who, exactly, you're *related* to—"

"Demons are not born," Aguillard said, sounding exhausted by the prospect of explaining it once again. "We are eruptions, manifestations of knowledge and power that evolve as further knowledge and power are gained. That Delphine and I manifested from the same eruption is not relation."

"The other creatures might not feel the same way," Jack warned.

Aguillard sat back in his chair, observing him, while Jack silently hoped his gamble—that knowing Aguillard's connection to Delphine LaLaurie might turn all of New Orleans against him—would pay off. After all, against one man, a demon was all but unconquerable; against an entire community of creatures, not so much.

"Well," Aguillard mused, steepling his fingers at his lips, "if you've grown tired of keeping my secret, Jack, then I suppose we'll have to do something about that, won't we?"

Damn, Jack thought grimly.

Gambling with a demon was always much too steep a risk.

Unsurprisingly, Elisabeth's sisters were growing unsettled in their confinement. Louisa, the romance author, was having a perfectly normal time continuing to write her stories as she always had, but the others, who were long accustomed to their nighttime hunts for unsuspecting mortals, were growing restless. Worse, they were getting hungry, and hangry groups of women who happened to be the vengeful undead were no better than the mortal kind.

"Have you found anything?" Jeanie asked Elisabeth impatiently that morning. "You've been poring over the alchemist's journal for weeks."

"I told you it wouldn't have anything useful," Genevieve added, approaching Elisabeth's desk. "Jack knows better than to write down anything you could use. Particularly," she said, flipping the leather book closed, much to Elisabeth's annoyance, "seeing as he probably knew you'd steal it the moment he told you it existed."

The unfortunate truth was that what Elisabeth *actually* needed was Jack's expertise. His knowledge of alchemy, all four centuries of it, *and* his particular capacity for figuring out how to stay alive when so many creatures had come for his head. She needed to ask him questions, but seeing as the last thing he'd done was try to murder her under the cover of night, she didn't particularly feel it would be a fruitful conversation.

"I told you, I have a plan," Elisabeth said, and Genevieve rolled her eyes.

"Convincing the Caretaker to kill Jack so the blacklist is lost to anarchy isn't a *plan*," she said. "It's at best an aspiration."

"Well, it's important to set achievable goals," Elisabeth sniffed, hunting through her collection of wigs and choosing a short, bright platinum one. Anyone who saw her would require a second glance to recognize her, but they wouldn't get one; she'd be gone before her identity had time to process. "I'll be away no more than half an hour," she said, warning the others. "Don't leave until I get back."

The others grumbled, of course, as they usually did, but Elisabeth slipped out and made her way to the Caretaker's house, watching from the outside to see if anyone else was coming or going. She could feel that Jack wasn't home; he usually left noticeable traces. After a few minutes of waiting, she saw Marisa open the door and slip into the street, heading somewhere down Royal.

Elisabeth paused for a moment, observing Marisa
Marrero as she made her way through the French
Quarter's usual crowd. She had a solemnity to her, her
shoulders always slightly hunched as a consequence of
her height, but there was no denying the way she stood
out in a crowd. The amber of her eyes flicked through
the street's bustling occupants while Elisabeth stayed
carefully out of sight, waiting.

Then Marisa was gone, and Elisabeth made her way
into the house.

Locks never stood a chance against a vampire once
the vampire in question had been invited in, which
Elisabeth had been once, many years ago. Unbeknownst
to Marisa, the ownership of the house had never actually
changed hands. It did, of course, have a refillable
position of Caretaker, which had been Oscalia Marrero
for nearly seventy years. Before that, it was Cornelio, a
sycophantic idiot with a taste for liquor and women, who
had, for those same reasons, worshipped the ground
beneath Jack's feet.

But the house itself had been purchased by Jack St.
Germaine, who had been a fool for Elisabeth once. Just
as she'd unwisely been for him.

The house had calmed significantly since the time it
had first been purchased. No more were there elaborate

parties and women being pumped so full of opioids and magical elixirs that they leapt from windows screaming about men who drank their blood. In those days, Jack had kept a rowdy crowd, always surrounded by the types of creatures irresponsibly bathed in the luxury of their twisted consumption, and it had been his undoing.

In the end, it had been Elisabeth's very great pleasure to have him banished, cheerfully forcing him into hiding. Since then, he'd been careful not to cause much damage, rarely staying in the city for more than a few days at a time. She couldn't even remember the last time she'd seen Jack use much magic aside from the occasional parlor trick—minus her own near-fatal attack.

She wandered inside the house, uncertain what she was looking for, but also positive that whatever she needed to find, it probably existed here. Elisabeth's instincts were highly refined, cultivated from being a highly niche carnivore along with a natural sense of what might yield promising results. She wandered into the library, poring over Jack's books and opening them individually, flipping aimlessly through the contents.

She was turning the page in a collection of night-growing defensive plants when another book suddenly toppled to the ground, narrowly missing her feet. She stepped quickly out of the way, glancing up, but there was nothing. No one.

"Hello?" she said.

Another book toppled from the shelf to the floor, falling open.

Elisabeth bent down, glancing over her shoulder and scanning the room again. No movement. She turned her attention to the page, adjusting her platinum wig slightly and glancing over the passage.

...the term 'unfinished business' is among one of the most widely used when applied to malevolent spirits, though there is of course the rare case of the benign. Untimely death, usually the result of homicide, is the most common cause for paranormal activity, and in the majority of cases the spirit, creature or otherwise, will ultimately find themselves on a pilgrimage back to the site of their final hours...

Elisabeth stopped, looking up.

"Oscalia?" she asked, and perhaps she imagined it, but she felt a shuddering sigh of relief.

Aguillard stepped out of his office to bump into an unexpected presence.

"Oh, sorry," exhaled the Caretaker, Marisa Marrero. She stepped back with a hurried flush, adding, "I was looking for Jack." She hesitated, and then, "Have you seen him?"

A little swirl of discomfort arose in her mind at registering Aguillard's presence (unsurprising), followed by some particularly intimate glimpses of Jack and Elisabeth. A spark of longing alighted on the faces of both the alchemist and the Casket Girl, coloring them both a lovely, falsely blurred shade of rose.

The faint hint of guilt tinting the edges of what Aguillard recognized as memories rather than imaginings was unmistakable, and he quickly fought a laugh.

"Well," he remarked. "Quite a lovely tangle you're in, isn't it?"

Marisa gave him a hard grimace. "Has anyone ever told you it's rude to pry?"

"More than once, actually," he said, and she turned with a scowl, heading out of the bar. "Ah, Miss Marrero," he called after her. "Tell me, have you noticed anything different lately? Any new... sensations," he murmured. "Or the like?"

She cast a brief look of loathing over her shoulder at him.

"Why is it I always seem to run into you?" she said irritably. "I swear, other than you, the creatures who show up at my door never reappear to bother me ag-"

She broke off, blinking, and troublingly, Aguillard spotted something forming clearly, weightily, in her head.

It was an idea. A realization.

The creatures who check in never check out.

She blinked.

Death by your own hand, or by the creatures you will have wronged—

A memory.

If you do not claim your life yourself, then we will claim it for you—

The thought replayed a few times, spliced and reverted and reworked.

—the creatures you will have wronged—

—if you do not claim your life yourself—

Then, at the tail end,

Have to be careful with mind-reading. Multiple creatures are capable of it. Some fae, the occasional Japanese monster, demons...

Demons.

Her mind snagged on the concept and wrapped around it, pulled taut.

"If you see Jack, tell him I'm looking for him," Marisa said, hurrying to the stairs and darting up them.

Aguillard, meanwhile, watched her go in silence and frowned, disappointed to realize his plans would now be on quite an escalated timetable.

After waiting days for Elisabeth to venture away from the convent, Jack finally spotted her coming, blonde wig and all, and leapt to reach her before she could dart out of sight. "Elisabeth, please, just listen to me—"

Her first posture was combative, defensive. He hastily threw his hands in the air, palms up.

"I'm not an idiot," he said.

"I beg to differ," she replied.

She gave him a swift, scrutinizing glance and then, upon noticing he wasn't bearing any sort of wooden stake, paused long enough to narrow her dark gaze at him. "If you're going to kill me, Jack, you'll have to do it another day," she advised, with the drawling tone that meant she was displeased, but not particularly violent. Unsettled, maybe; wary, at best. "I've had a very trying day and I don't wish to worsen it with undue muscle strain."

"Just hear me out, Elisabeth, please—"

"Is this about Marisa?" Elisabeth prompted impatiently, and Jack frowned at her, bemused. "Because if you want to have her to yourself, Jack, that's hardly something to take up with me. You can't keep her from coming to me every time you've proven another disappointment, and you certainly can't try to kill me and then come to me for help."

"No, I—" He broke off, shaking his head in confusion; whatever this had to do with Marisa, he couldn't begin to guess. "I needed to tell you about Aguillard," he said, stepping closer in the hopes his urgency might compel her to listen. "I know we've been through a lot, and I know I've wronged you. But at the end of the day, Elisabeth, you trust me. You know you do," he implored her, pleading directly to her look of skepticism. "No matter our differences, you know I never really aim to hurt you."

"That's completely false. How many times have you sent someone after me, Jack?" she retorted, and he winced. It wasn't exactly untrue, though he'd never actually expected anyone to be better than she was. They were more like... obstacles. Warnings.

Violent ones, but still. "I never sent anyone *good*—"

"Oh yeah?" she scoffed. "Then how do you explain the attack in the middle of the night, hm? That could have only been your work—"

"Not true. Mine," Jack said, cutting in swiftly, "*or a* demon's."

She waved a hand, dismissive. "One and the same, as far as I'm concerned—"

"Are you listening to me? I said a *demon*—"

"Yes, and…?"

"Elisabeth, for god's sake," Jack growled, frustrated. She scowled in response, obviously prepared to launch a snide retort, but he rushed to add, "It *was* a demon, Elisabeth. Specifically Aguillard."

"Aguillard?" She frowned. "That can't be right."

"It is. And what's worse is that I couldn't have attacked you that night even if I wanted to. Though," Jack scoffed, "it's not as if you haven't earned it, sending Ilias after Marisa—"

Elisabeth's dark eyes narrowed in frustration. "I didn't send Ilias after anyone," she snarled, white teeth glinting, "and what do you mean you couldn't have done it?"

"I—" Jack paused, catching the sound of footsteps, and realized that if anyone—particularly Genevieve or one of the other Casket Girls—were to hear him, this conversation would be over before he even arrived at the point. "The demon I killed in Paris," he said quickly, rushing to summarize. "Delphine LaLaurie? I ended up with some of her powers. Demons don't die like other creatures do," he explained, and Elisabeth rolled her eyes.

"Don't mansplain creature lore to me, Jack, I *am* one—"

"Fine, whatever. The point is Aguillard is Delphine's... well, let's just call them twins," Jack said. At Elisabeth's frown of confusion, he went on, "Delphine's death meant I ended up with some of her powers, but I can't control them. The house—the Caretaker's house, with the Caretaker's power—that was an accident."

In retrospect, 'Caretaker' was a foolish title for the mistake he'd made, unintentionally turning the Marrero bloodline into a living talisman as a result of his own leaking powers. The name Caretaker had, at first, been a flimsy effort to make it sound like anything but.

"I didn't *mean* for it to happen, but..."

He held up his hands, trailing off, and Elisabeth blinked, startled. "Jack. Are you serious? If your power was *unintentionally* tied to the house, that's an enormous fucking accident."

"I know." He rubbed his temple, restless. "The powers I got from Delphine, Aguillard's power, they're tied to the same source. He followed it here to find me; the stronger he gets, the less I can control my own. I couldn't have come after you," he confessed with a shake of his head, "just like I can't stop him now. And if I'd ever tried telling anyone before—"

"He'd kill you, obviously." Like always, Elisabeth caught on quickly. "But surely you're more useful to him alive? Every creature in the city would come for him if they knew what he was."

Jack shook his head. "Apparently I'm not useful anymore," he said, and a flicker of concern passed over Elisabeth's contemplative features. "It used to be that he kept to the shadows, passing me off as the one in control. But I'm only getting weaker, and eventually people are bound to notice—"

"So why come to me?" Elisabeth demanded. "This is damning information. I could easily call for the blacklist to be turned on you."

"Yes. I know."

"You withheld information about a *demon*, Jack. And one that shares powers with Delphine LaLaurie, who terrorized this entire fucking city!"

"I know, believe me, I know."

Elisabeth began to pace in a slow circle, thinking in muttered silence.

"How," she determined after a moment, glancing up at Jack. "How is Aguillard getting more powerful?"

He shook his head. "I don't know. But he must have been able to manipulate Ilias somehow, and obviously he tried to attack you—"

"Oscalia," Elisabeth said, and it was Jack's turn to frown with confusion. "She's a ghost, Jack. And she's still in the house, I felt her."

"What? How could you possibly know th-"

"Your locks are flimsy." A lie, probably, but hardly at issue. "Just trust me, I know." Elisabeth paced a few more times, grimly lifting her gaze to Jack's. "If Aguillard killed Oscalia in the house where your power resides, what would that do to him?"

"I—" Jack broke off, thinking about it. "I don't know," he said, a bit startled that he didn't. "The house has magic concentrated in it; that's what the Caretaker gets."

Elisabeth nodded. "Yes."

"And it increases—"

"More with every creature who stays there, yes, I know." Principles of magic were hardly secret.

"Delphine played with mortal lives," Jack said, frowning. "She wouldn't have gotten anything from them. But the Caretaker—"

"Isn't a mortal. Not entirely. Which means—"

Elisabeth looked up at Jack, mouth set in a thin, grim line.

"Why should I trust you?" she told him. "You've betrayed me, Jack, time and time again."

He opened his mouth. Closed it. "So have you."

"Right," she said brusquely, "so why should we work together now?"

"Because—" He grimaced, not particularly willing to say it, and Elisabeth folded her arms over her chest, waiting expectantly. "Are you really going to make me say it?"

She arched a brow.

"Fine," Jack muttered, glaring at her, and the thin corners of her mouth slid up, darkly satisfied. "Because I need you, Elisabeth. You're better than me. Stronger." She eyed her fingernails, the very portrait of conceit. "There's a reason I could never be rid of you, even when I wanted to," he continued, a gritted confession, "but this time, I swear, I mean it. I need you."

There must have been something in his voice; she looked up, brows furrowed.

"Elisabeth, please." He swallowed, and then, "I really can't do this alone."

There was a long silence that followed. Elisabeth had never been easy to predict; for a long time, she looked as if she was still equally torn between helping him and killing him, and there was no telling which one she'd choose.

Though, he hoped he knew.

Foolishly, he hoped.

"I told you you'd gone soft," she said after a long minute. Jack rolled his eyes, regrettably accepting that as something of a truce, but the thought seemed to have taken her to a more pressing conclusion.

"Does Aguillard already know you can't stop him?"

There it was: The Problem.

Jack nodded once, slowly, and Elisabeth's eyes fell shut, and then open.

"Then we have to get to Marisa right now," she said, taking off without another word.

When Aguillard arrived at the Caretaker's house, Marisa was waiting for him. She sat on the stairs, wordless, as he opened the door.

"So. You're not a vampire," Marisa said, her voice hollow and dull.

Aguillard shook his head. "No," he confirmed, watching her stiffen in response. "And I must say, I'm pleased you were able to arrive at that conclusion, though I doubt it will make a difference either way."

He could sense that a little seed of something was in her head now that they were in her house; whatever it was, it seemed to be newly taking root. He tried to probe it, to understand what it was or how it had been planted, but it only seemed to glow more fully, refracting to obscure itself with a shield he couldn't quite interpret.

"I checked the rooms. They're empty." Marisa rose to her feet, one hand on the stairway railing. Her thoughts around the seedling of an idea were unusually calm; more placid than vacant, but he could feel the thrumming vibration of something that oscillated between conviction and anger. "The creatures who check in never check out, do they? You make sure of it."

"What would that matter to you?" Aguillard asked her, shrugging. "I thought you didn't particularly care for this role."

"I don't." It was growing roots, spindly tendrils. It was securing itself in her head, implantation in the earth of what she was. The earth itself was a fixture in her

193

mind; she seemed conscious of it beneath her feet, and the tremble of her thoughts grew volatile, even seismic. "But that doesn't mean I like what you're doing."

"And what am I doing?" If that was a taunt, so be it. He slid beyond the boundaries of his corporeal form, trickling out of himself. He could turn pain up and down like a dial. He could invade her somewhere she couldn't prevent, or even predict. He'd gone easy on Elisabeth Clavier the night he'd attacked her, wanting only to anger her; to frustrate her enough to keep her from turning to Jack. But for Marisa Marrero, Aguillard could make her state of existence so supremely uncomfortable that the life force inside her would simply implode within its container, consumed by the pressure of what little she was.

"You're killing them," Marisa said. Most likely she was seeing his form begin to warp, the way Ilias' had. But she didn't have Jack to save her this time, and Ilias had been old, weak, easily manipulated. Ilias had been draining out, devolving, but Aguillard was only earning, gaining strength from the sacrifices he had made. "You think it's making you more powerful, don't you? But you can't control everything; you didn't even know what Ilias actually said to me. You sent him here without knowing what prophecy he'd eventually deliver."

The mention of Ilias caught his attention briefly. "What difference does Ilias' message make?"

"Oh, only everything." The seed in her mind had begun to expel in branches, the roots embedded now. "The creatures I wronged... I know who they are now. I'm the Caretaker," she spat at Aguillard, "and that means something, doesn't it?"

Idiot girl. Overly emotional, like all of them. "The first Caretaker was little more than a cuckold," Aguillard told her, deciding to invade her mind with it, watching her wince at the screeching sound in her head. "A brainless disciple of Jack St. Germaine's, put in place to absorb the excess when his powers could not be controlled. Don't you understand you are merely beholden to Jack's error? There is no higher calling to be found," he snarled at her. "This is merely irresponsible magic, and you are nothing but an alchemist's tool."

"Maybe I would have been, if not for you," Marisa permitted, and whatever it was, it was flowering now, shoving him out. Aguillard tried to grasp the mortal core of her, the same feeble weakness that had so easily undone what was left of Oscalia, but this time—to his astonishment—he couldn't find it. It had been filled, instead, by something else.

By power even the Caretaker should not have had.

Marisa shoved him out, expelling him until he rattled within his own form, ricocheting back into his own container.

"What is this?" Aguillard demanded, feeling his edges pulse and wane. "What are you doing?"

Marisa Marrero, the new Caretaker, let out a little laugh.

"This is why Ilias' message matters. Because if I do not claim my life myself," she began, and in response, Aguillard felt a crackling inside him, shattering like glass.

—then we will claim it for you.

It was easier than she thought it would be, as if some invisible hand had lain itself maternally on her shoulder and in response, all Marisa had to do was allow herself to be guided. The rumble beneath her feet seemed to rise in waves, licking at her fingertips, and when all that was required of her was to give it permission, to acquiesce, she said: *Claim me, then.*

With the power manifesting from the house, cracking the floorboards and splintering the walls, the low sense of chatter that had been living on the outskirts of her mind was finally invited in. The very simple idea—*I failed you, so take what you need*—became, for once, the easiest, most thoughtless thing to access. Not learned in a book or probed through countless questions, but simply the invitation: Have it, whatever it is. Let me be the instrument of your choosing.

It was a blur, whatever happened next; the foreign, disembodied sense of rage that overtook her. The betrayal, the tiny, festering cataclysms and bursts of power that couldn't be erased bound Aguillard to his own bones, chained to the weakness of his human form.

It was all going to be used up, eradicated by virtue of its creation; the effort expended to trap Aguillard within himself, turning the collective source of his power inward, was like the death of a binary star; a spectacular collision. It would crumple in on itself and, in the same token, eject itself into nothing, created by what it had destroyed.

Death by your own hand, or by the creatures you will have wronged—

Aguillard let out a scream, or something like one, an intense flash illuminating before Marisa's eyes; a collapsing supernova, bright and blinding as the power that had filled her exploded outwards, hollowing her out until she was nothing but a vacuum of mortality.

Nothing, except for earthly tunnels of veins, blood and bone.

Tricky demon, Marisa thought, the chatter in her head gradually falling silent.

Death was only another word for annihilation.

Jack and Elisabeth were standing at a distance when Royal Street had suddenly been flooded with a blinding, deafening explosion. They blinked away the lightning-bolt of pressure, struggling to regain what had not been damaged of their vision, and both took off at a run, the ringing in their ears slowly fading as Jack shoved open the house's door.

"Marisa," he said, running to her, but Elisabeth paused in the doorway, sensing something hollow in the air. It was a vacancy where there had been something larger, possibly even something massive. The enormity of the sudden emptiness was slightly eerie, disruptive. Elisabeth frowned, feeling around for Jack's usual enchantments, and discovered...

Nothing. She ran a finger over the panels of the threshold, marveling silently at its mundanity.

The wood was only wood.

Gradually, the deadness of it made her shiver, suffering a little tremor of portent. She repelled it back, turning away, and caught Marisa's gaze where it had been cast over Jack's shoulder.

"Are you alright?" Jack said in Marisa's ear, stroking her hair gently, but she didn't answer.

Her amber eyes were sharp, alarmingly focused; wolfish. Predatory. It was a look Elisabeth knew troublingly well, and amid the prickling unease of her misgivings, Elisabeth did what she had so often said she'd never do: she listened for the sound of Marisa's thoughts.

It didn't take long to find the thought in question. The voice in Marisa's head was clear, ringing like a bell.

I'm ready to take my life back, it said, floating weightless until it secured itself like an anchor.

Elisabeth blinked, half-leaping forward.

"No, Marisa, don't—!"

But Marisa had already closed her fingers around the handle of Jack's knife, pulling it free from his belt and then shoving it, forcefully, into his chest, sending him staggering to his knees with a hard, earth-shaking drop.

Elisabeth froze, unsure what to do; where to go.

"Marisa," Jack gasped, but she held tightly to the handle, securing it there in his heart.

"Sorry, Jack," Marisa said, wiping her sweat-slicked curls from her cheeks, her wild eyes. "Nothing personal. These living arrangements just aren't working for me."

He tried to answer; probably to plead, but as Elisabeth already knew from experience, mortal men never managed to say much at all once they'd started bleeding in earnest. She supposed she shouldn't have been surprised that even alchemists who had lived through four centuries, limitless identities, and countless love affairs still fell to their deaths the same way.

Elisabeth's hand rose to her mouth in silence as she watched Jack St. Germaine fall limply to one side. His blue eyes, vacant and lost by the time Marisa finally released him, stared glassily into nothing as Marisa rose slowly to her feet, turning to Elisabeth.

"Happy now?" Marisa asked her, and Elisabeth blinked.

Blinked again.

"Did you…"

But the numbness of Jack's death crept into the arrhythmic hum of Elisabeth's pulse, rendering her unable to finish the sentence.

"Did I kill Aguillard, too?" Marisa guessed. "Yes."

"But—"

Please, Elisabeth. I need you.

Elisabeth curled her hand to a fist, digging her nails into her palm as Marisa yanked the knife from Jack's chest, freeing it. She underwent the few long strides it took to reach Elisabeth, who remained still across the room, and then Marisa held the knife at arm's length, aiming the blade at the neckline of Elisabeth's black dress.

For a moment they both simply stood there, eyeing each other in silence.

"Did you even love me?" Marisa asked eventually, and in response, Elisabeth looked down at the knife.

Stared at it.

Then looked up at Marisa.

"I don't know," Elisabeth said dully. "I've never known if I was even capable."

Marisa's mouth twitched, then stilled.

She raised the knife, and Elisabeth held her breath.

Then Marisa twisted it around, offering her the handle, and Elisabeth exhaled, accepting it.

She watched, wordless, as Marisa moved purposefully around the room, stepping over Jack's unmoving form and picking up her purse, turning to look over her shoulder.

"Sorry," Marisa said. "But you get it, right?"

Elisabeth shrugged. "You have to do what it takes to be free," she said.

They exchanged a single nod, conspiratorial in their agreement.

Then, without another word, Marisa exited the house's front door, shutting it behind her and leaving Elisabeth to stare down at the knife in her hand, the smell of Jack's blood slowly filling up her senses.

Leese, Marisa texted her sister, *I'm at the airport. I get into BOS in a few hours.*

Alicia's response was instantaneous: *What? OMG that's great news, I've missed you so much! How long are you staying?*

Marisa considered it, then shook her head. *Honestly? I've had enough NOLA to last me a lifetime. I'm coming home,* she said simply, and tucked her phone back in her purse, knowing she wasn't in the mood to answer Alicia's questions quite yet.

As she replaced her phone, Marisa brushed the pages of the book she'd forgotten she'd left floating around inside her bag. She pulled it out to eye the cover before flipping back through the pages, finding a dog-eared page close to the end.

"Will we ever find each other again, Jacques?"

"Always, Elisabeth. I do not know how to exist without you."

"What a load of crap," Marisa scoffed, tossing the book in the garbage.

Then she looked up at the departure board, locating her gate, and headed down the corridor, leaving New Orleans and all of its lore behind her.

The ghost watched in silence as the dark-haired girl bent over Jack St. Germaine's body, rising to slide a pearl of blood from the side of her unpainted lips. He choked awake with a gasp, struggling to fill his lifeless lungs, and the Casket Girl, Elisabeth Clavier, gruffly took hold of the back of his head, raising it to the side of her own neck.

"Drink," she said, and winced only slightly when he must have permitted himself to sink his teeth into her skin, drawing blood with a visible shudder. "Oi. Relax," she scolded him, rolling her eyes as she settled herself in a more comfortable position, one hand still curled around the nape of his neck. "No better time than the present to learn control," she murmured, tapping a careful pattern along his vertebrae and slowly, very slowly, channeling her pain into a controlled meditation of breaths.

It took another minute or so before Jack gradually detached himself from her skin, scraping the back of his hand across his crimson-stained mouth.

He stared at Elisabeth silently, brow furrowing as he licked her from his lips.

"Why?" he said eventually, and she shrugged.

"I don't know," she said, not quite meeting his eye. "I guess you've just been part of my world so long that I'm not sure how to exist without trying to kill you in it."

Oscalia watched, curious, as a slow smile spread across Jack's face.

"Some 'two sides of the same coin' bullshit, Lise?"

"Yeah, something like that. Jacques."

They sat together in silence again; a different silence than before, and in that precise moment, a soft, rosy glow illuminated beside Oscalia, beckoning to her with hazy, hovering tendrils of light.

She turned, reaching out with the tips of her fingers, and felt the warmth of its summons curling around her skin. Tentatively, she walked towards it, one foot in front of the other, until the yawning too-brightness swallowed her up and delivered her to the other side, leaving her with a sense of calm, unerring peace.

Then, somehow, amid all the brilliance, Oscalia managed to open her eyes.

It had always been like waking from a dream.

THE END

Olivie Blake

ABOUT *the* AUTHOR

Olivie Blake is a lover and writer of stories, many of which involve the fantastic, the paranormal, or the supernatural, but not always. More often, her works revolve around what it means to be human (or not), and the endlessly interesting complexities of life and love.

Olivie has been published as the featured fiction contributor for Witch Way Magazine, as well as the writer for the graphic series *Alpha*, the anthologies *Fairytales of the Macabre, Midsummer Night Dreams*, and *The Lovers Grim*, and the novels *Masters of Death, Lovely Tangled Vices*, and *One For My Enemy*. She lives and works in Los Angeles, where she is generally tolerated by her rescue pit bull.

9 780578 555201